TIME FOR A LITTLE FUN

Depuy came running out of the darkness, a dagger in one hand. Raider danced out of the way of the gambler's frenzied first thrust. For a moment he was tempted to draw his pistol and put a bullet through Depuy's gut, but the past few days had been boring; it was time for a little fun. Raider reached across his body and drew his bowie.

Depuy lunged at Raider, but Raider parried easily and brought his bowie down hard against Depuy's knife. There was a ringing of steel against steel and Depuy's blade broke. The gambler looked down at what was left of his weapon, and licked his lips. "You—you wouldn't kill an unarmed man, would you?" he rasped.

Other books in the RAIDER series by
J. D. HARDIN

HIGHWAY
OF DEATH

B
BERKLEY BOOKS, NEW YORK

HIGHWAY OF DEATH

A Berkley Book/published by arrangement with
the author

PRINTING HISTORY
Berkley edition/November 1989

ISBN: 0-425-11839-8

A BERKLEY BOOK® TM 757,375
Berkley Books are published by The Berkley Publishing Group,
200 Madison Avenue, New York, New York 10016.
The name ''BERKLEY'' and the ''B'' logo
are trademarks belonging to Berkley Publishing Corporation.

PRINTED IN THE UNITED STATES OF AMERICA

10 9 8 7 6 5 4 3 2 1

CHAPTER ONE

The town was named Caliente. It was a name that fit, Caliente being a Spanish word that means hot, and hot it was: hot and dry and dusty, not only in the town, but throughout the surrounding countryside as well. The land shimmered under an oppressive heat that rose from hard-baked earth. To the north, the terrain was flat and featureless, stretching away toward a distant horizon distorted by heat haze. Steep barren mountains formed a wall toward the south. It was definitely not a land of milk and honey.

The stranger rode in from the north, a tall man on a tall horse. The heat shimmer distorted both horse and rider; if you were far enough away, they looked a little bent to one side. A drunk, hunkered down against the boardwalk in front of the saloon he'd just been thrown out of, watched horse and rider grow larger and straighter as they approached. Anything to take his mind off all that whiskey inside the saloon. Whiskey currently out of his reach. He was broke.

At first he took the rider for a saddle tramp. His rather plain clothing had been turned a uniform dun color by dust. Dust rimmed the crown and brim of his hat. Even his horse was dusty.

But as the rider drew level with the saloon, the drunk, who in better days had been a man of some consequence and

1

intelligence, noticed that the horse was a very fine animal, a tall bay stallion that appeared to be in excellent condition. So did the rider. He was a big man, broad across the shoulders and lean in the waist. His bandanna, dusty as it was, appeared to be made of silk, and his boots exhibited the elegant simplicity of fine hand-crafted leather.

But it was the rider's weapons that most commanded the drunk's attention. A Colt revolver with polished walnut grips hung low on the rider's right hip. The drunk noticed that the top of the holster had been partially cut away, giving easier access to the revolver's butt, hammer, and trigger. A gunfighter's rig. And the rifles; there were two of them, their smooth, polished butts jutting from snug-fitting saddle scabbards. The drunk recognized one of the rifles as a Winchester; the other was probably a big-bore Sharps. The rider was a mobile arsenal, down to the big bowie knife that rode in a sheath toward his left side.

The drunk hesitated, kicking around the idea of hitting up this stranger for the price of a drink. Perhaps the stranger read his thoughts. He turned his head and looked straight at the drunk. The rider's face was lean and rather handsome, bisected by a thick moustache, but it was his eyes that the drunk noticed most; black, very black eyes, of a piercing intensity that seemed to look right through him. The drunk looked away. This was not the kind of man from whom one cadged drinks.

The stranger rode on by, heading toward a dilapidated wooden building with a sign over its front door that read, "Wells Fargo and Company." He swung down from the saddle, stretched stiff legs for a moment, then tied his horse's reins to the hitching rail. Hands free, he arched his back and stretched his entire body. Joints cracked. The man shook himself, loosening saddle-sore muscles; then he finally stepped up onto the boardwalk and went in through the building's front door.

There was more room inside than he'd expected; room enough for a counter near the door, screening off an area filled by three desks. Two doors toward the rear of the room indicated more space behind.

A clerk was seated behind one of the desks. He looked up at the stranger from beneath his green-tinted eyeshade. His manner was supercilious at first, as he took in the dusty, trail-worn clothing—until he noticed the eyes. "Yes sir?" he said, quickly getting to his feet. "Can I help you?"

"I'm lookin' for James Hume. He in?"

"Why, yes sir." The clerk's eyes swiveled toward one of the doors at the back of the room. "Who shall I say is calling?"

"Raider."

The clerk stood waiting. When nothing followed, he asked, "Is that all, sir? Just Raider?"

"Just Raider."

The clerk shrugged, then went over and knocked on the door, opened it a crack, and called inside, once again just a trifle superciliously, "A Mister Raider to see you, Mister Hume."

Raider heard chair legs scrape against a wooden floor, then a moment later the door opened all the way and a tall, well set up man with neatly-combed graying hair, and a large sweeping moustache stepped out into the main room. "Raider!" he said. "We didn't think you were coming. The railroad men have been meeting all the trains for the past week."

"I d'cided t' ride. I was over on the coast. Came in from Paso Robles."

"Ah—because of the robberies over that way."

"Yep. I'd still be there 'cept the agency ordered me t' come here. Cain't say I'm too happy 'bout it. Hate t' leave a job half done. Hell. I wasn't even that far along."

Hume nodded. Raider noticed that he had very fine eyes, of a light gray color. Eyes that looked straight at a man. He'd never met Hume before, but he respected his reputation. Hume was chief of detectives for the Wells Fargo Express Company. A man didn't hold down a job like that by being a fool. "Well," Hume said, "we have a problem here, too.

The railroad asked your agency to send their best man. I put up your name; I've heard a thing or two about the way you work, so I guess I get the blame for you being here.''

"Hell of a place."

Hume nodded. "I can't disagree with that. But the rails go through where they can."

A dull rolling thud shook the building. Hume smiled. "Hear that? They're blasting their way through the Tehachapis just a few miles farther along. The rails will reach Los Angeles within the year, with or without these troubles we've been having."

" 'Fraid I don't know much 'bout that."

"Come on into my office. I'll fill you in."

Hume waved Raider in through the door from which he'd just exited. There was nothing inside but a desk and a couple of chairs, all of which had a thin film of the inevitable local dust. Hume sat behind the desk. Raider took a chair facing him. He noticed that there was very little on top of the desk, indeed, very little in the office to show permanent residency. Obviously this was just a temporary place for Hume to hang his hat.

Hume leaned back in his chair. Raider heard wood creak. "Robberies," Hume said. "Lots or robberies. Stages, ranch houses, travelers, even a couple of trains have been hit."

"Sure," Raider interjected. "Railroads mean money. Every small-time drifter who wants a stake will be gravitatin' to this area."

"We're not too worried about the small-timers," Hume replied. "Sure, we have occasional trouble from men like that, but most of the robberies, the big ones, the ones that hurt, seem to be the work of a single gang, or a group of gangs. We've had a number of obviously organized robberies, carried out with speed and efficiency. And they're causing the railroad, and Wells Fargo, and a lot of other people, a great deal of grief. Wells Fargo intends to stop these robberies. And so does the railroad."

"Ah," Raider said, grinning for the first time. "The Big

Four. I s'pose I'm workin' for 'em. I s'pose the whole damned country's gonna end up workin' for them four yahoos.''

Hume looked at Raider from beneath his eyebrows. ''I gather you don't like them.''

Raider didn't answer directly. ''The Big Four. I wonder what would've happened if they'd stayed storekeepers.''

''For one thing, we wouldn't have a railroad out here,'' Hume replied acerbically. ''Is your dislike of the Big Four going to affect the way you work, Raider?''

Raider looked straight at Hume. ''Naw. I'm a practical man. I don't like robbers of any kind, but since there's not much point in goin' after robber barons, I'll take on plain robbers.''

Hume was about to say something else, but he was distracted by a great deal of noise from outside: the thunder of hooves, the rattle of wheels, and one hell of a lot of excited shouting. Hume leaped up from his chair and was already through the door and into the main room when a dusty man came rushing in through the street door. The man looked around wildly, then spotted Hume. ''Mr. Hume!'' he burst out. The bastards have gone an' done it again—robbed the northbound stage outta Los Angeles!''

CHAPTER TWO

Raider, standing in the doorway of Hume's office, could see, through a small window, a stagecoach out in the street in front of the office. Men were milling about near the coach. He could hear their excited chatter. Meanwhile, Hume was trying to calm the excited man who'd burst into the room. "Slow down, Burt," Hume snapped. "Tell me exactly what happened."

"I just did!" Burt snapped back. "Road agents. They held us up 'bout four, five miles outside town. Ran off with the strongbox."

Hume appeared to be cool, although Raider thought he could detect a whitening around his eyes that indicated suppressed anger. "How many of them?" Hume asked Burt, who Raider assumed must be the stage's driver.

"Two. One had a shotgun, the other a pistol. Got us on a blind curve, where we had to slow the horses to a walk. One minute there wasn't nobody around but us, the next minute I was lookin' down both barrels o' what had to be a ten bore. The other one was on the other side, coverin' Tom. No way Tom could bring his rifle around in time to get 'em both, afore they got at least one of us."

"No matter," Hume replied. I don't think there was much in the stongbox, but we'll get after those two gents anyhow."

He turned toward the clerk with the green eyeshade. "Go over to the marshall's office. Ask him to round up a posse—a dozen men. We should be mounted, armed, and ready to ride within twenty minutes."

As the clerk ran outside to order up the posse, Raider walked over to the excited driver. "You said four or five miles outta town?" he asked.

"Yep."

"Describe the place. Could I find it easy?"

The driver scratched his head. "Well, sure. There's a big rock that kinda sticks right out into the road, with a smaller rock on the other side. Then there's a big tree with a missin' top, maybe blasted off by lightnin'. That's where they hit us. One of 'em come out from behind that big rock, the other one—"

"I get the picture," Raider said, cutting off the flow of excited chatter. He walked around the man and headed toward the door. "Are you going out alone?" Hume called after him.

"Yep. My horse is standin' right outside, saddled an' ready t' ride. I can be on the trail o' those two yahoos before they get very far."

Hume made no effort to dissuade him. "Good luck. We'll be along after you."

A few minutes later Raider was astride his mount and headed out of town, south. The road was quite broad at first, designed to carry the supplies that were needed at the railhead. There was considerable traffic; wagons loaded with tools, workmen on foot, an occasional rider. Within a few minutes the land became more rolling. Arid foothills led up into equally arid mountains. There were scattered trees on the slopes, mostly dwarf oak. Off to the left, Raider could see the raw gouges in the hillsides where engineers were building a series of looping rights of way that would permit the rail line to maintain an easy grade up through the mountains. The wagon road he was on diverged about a mile farther along, bearing off to the right, headed toward the pass that began the long stage route toward Los Angeles and the rest of southern California.

Once past the railhead, the road was deserted. Raider had no trouble at all finding the place where the stage had been held up. The driver's description had been accurate. There was a huge rock on one side of the trail, a smaller rock on the other side, and a lightning-blasted tree just above the road. The stage would have had to come nearly to a stop here, to negotiate a sharp turn in the trail around that huge rock. It was not difficult to visualize the bandits coming out from behind the rocks, shoving their weapons into the faces of the startled driver and guard, then demanding that the strongbox be thrown down. Raider could see the mark of boot heels in the soft dirt near the edge of the road.

There were other marks there too, sharp angles in the dirt that had undoubtedly been made when the heavy metal strongbox had been thrown down from the stage. Dismounting, Raider went over to where the marks were the most noticeable, near the edge of the road. Here, they'd been gouged in more deeply, as if the box had been moved back and forth. Something glittered in the sunlight, half-hidden by a patch of weeds. Raider bent down and picked up part of a knife blade. The rest of the blade and the handle were lying several yards away, half-buried in the dirt, as if someone had thrown them there with considerable force.

Raider could hardly believe it. The dumb bastards hadn't brought anything to open the strongbox. Usually, a well-prepared road agent brought along an ax or a sledgehammer, something big enough to burst open the box. Raider could imagine the robbers trying to pry it open with a knife, right here, alongside the road, right where they'd robbed the stage. Raider shrugged. Obviously a couple of amateurs.

Walking around behind the big boulder, he found hoofprints. The robbers were mounted, which might be good for him; they wouldn't be able to slip away up some narrow mountain path where a horse couldn't follow.

Tracks led away up a dry wash. Going back to where he'd

left his horse, Raider mounted, and began following the tracks. The two robbers hadn't done much to cover their trail, so Raider was able to follow at a steady trot. A mile farther along, the wash narrowed. Raider had to slow his mount. Now it was more difficult to make out the tracks, not because the robbers had been any more careful about covering the marks of their passage, but because the ground was harder, and more broken. Still, he was able to follow, but now at a slow walk. The robbers would be able to gain distance.

Farther ahead, the land was much more rugged. Steeply rising mountains were broken by deep gullies and canyons. There were few trees, but a lot of dry brush, which was difficult for a horse to penetrate. About two miles from the road, the bandits, who must have been having just as much trouble with the brush as Raider, had branched off the narrow trail they'd been following and headed up into one of the canyons. At this point, the canyon floor was fairly level, which was undoubtedly the reason the robbers had chosen it, but Raider could see that it would not remain that way. About a mile farther along, the canyon's rise into the mountains steepened. He nodded. He was indeed following a pair of amateurs. The route they had chosen would effectively channel them in a predetermined direction. There was no way they'd be able to change course now; the canyon walls were far too steep for a horse.

Reaching behind him, Raider pulled a pair of binoculars from his saddlebags. He sat his horse for several minutes, carefully studying the terrain ahead. What idiots. They should have headed off to the left, where the terrain, while rougher at the outset, was much easier farther along. The canyon they had chosen would eventually lead them in that direction anyhow, but after a lot of hard traveling.

Raider headed off to the left. At first it was difficult riding, but within a quarter mile he found the going easier, a gentle climb up into the mountains. He should have little trouble heading off the bandits; his route and their route would intersect about a mile ahead, and since he had easier riding, he would reach that point first.

A half hour later, Raider reached the point where the narrow upper section of the canyon route the robbers had taken rose over a crest and entered a shallow depression. The bandits would have to pass by this place to leave the canyon. From the absence of tracks, he could tell they had not yet come this far. Good. This was where he would take them.

Raider was looking around for a suitable ambush point when he heard the faint sound of hammering from back down the canyon. He stopped to listen. The sound continued. Several minutes later he could still hear it. Finally, Raider nudged his horse over the crest and started down into the canyon.

He'd only ridden half a mile when he found the two road agents. They were both dismounted, squatting beside the Wells Fargo strongbox, hammering at it with rocks. He could hear their sulfurous swearing as they pounded away. Apparently the box had been too heavy and bulky for them to continue carrying, so they were trying to open it now, when they should have been concentrating on putting as much distance as possible between themselves and the site of the robbery.

Raider quickly dismounted, and led his horse behind some stunted trees. Once again pulling out his binoculars, he lay on the ground behind some bushes and studied the two bandits. They did not look very impressive; two rather smallish, scrawny men, dressed in ragged clothing. A shotgun was propped against a rock several yards from where they were working. One of the men had what looked like an old cap and ball pistol stuck into his belt.

Returning to his horse, Raider mounted, then rode slowly down the canyon toward the two men, angling off to one side, taking a route that would keep him concealed from them for as long as possible. Fortunately, the sound of their increasingly desperate hammering was loud enough to cover the sound of his horse's hooves.

Raider was only thirty yards away from the two bandits,

sitting his horse next to some thick bushes, when the strong-box finally broke open. He heard a howl of triumph from one of the men, who immediately shoved his hand into the shattered box and began to pull out various papers. The other man crowded in close. "Where's the gold, Lige? I don't see no gold."

"Shit. There ain't any," the other man snarled. "Just a lotta letters, and this here thing. Looks like a check."

"Open the mail, Jethro," Lige whined. "Maybe there's money inside."

Jethro grunted his assent, but even as he was tearing open an envelope, Raider was easing his Winchester from its saddle scabbard. He saw Jethro waving a bank note in the air. "Five dollars," Jethro shouted. I found us five dollars."

"That's all?" Lige groused. "Five lousy dollars?"

Raider's voice broke into their conversation. "That five dollars will get you five years," he called out, at the same time levering a round into the Winchester's chamber.

It was difficult to tell what startled the two stagecoach robbers more; the unexpected sound of Raider's voice, or the terrible clanking of the rifle's action. Both Lige and Jethro leaped to their feet, staring around wildly before finally locating the source of the interruption. They found themselves staring straight down the muzzle of a rock-steady rifle. "Don't move a muscle, boys," Raider said quietly.

Lige, the one with the pistol, had one hand on its butt. Jethro was glancing toward his shotgun. But neither man moved. It was not just the rifle that stopped them, it was the calmness of Raider's voice, his obvious readiness to shoot them down if they made a hostile move.

Raider ordered Lige to remove his pistol from his belt with his left hand and throw it over near the shotgun. Moving with extreme care, Lige did so. Then Raider rode out into the little clearing and swung down from the saddle. Still keeping the men covered with his rifle, he removed some lengths of thin cord from his saddlebags. He had Lige tie Jethro's hands in front of him, then, propping his rifle against a bush, Raider tied Lige's hands. There was one short moment, as Raider was approaching Lige, when defiance, or desperation, or both, showed on the outlaw's face, but after a long look into Raider's eyes, he meekly held out his hands.

After both men had been tied, Raider gathered up the debris from the strongbox. There were letters, the check, and a few documents that he didn't bother to read. It had indeed been a poor haul, but as he'd said when he drew down on the two unlucky robbers, it would be enough to get them five years apiece in the state prison at San Quentin.

Raider made both men mount their horses. Then he tied their hands to their saddle horns. After attaching lead ropes to the bridles of the bandits' horses, Raider mounted. Taking the lead ropes in his left hand, he started back down the canyon, with Jethro and Lige trailing disconsolately after him.

After about a mile, Jethro finally spoke. "Mister," he said, "we ain't never done nothin' like this before."

"It shows," Raider replied laconically.

Encouraged by Raider's easy manner, Jethro began to speak hurriedly. "We was down in Los Angeles, runnin' damn low on luck. We'd tried some minin' up north, but got run out by those rich muckety-mucks who've been takin' over everythin'. Shit," he snorted, spitting disgustedly to one side, "in bad times like these, the small man ain't got the chance of a snowball in Hell."

Raider nodded. Since the big business collapse two years ago, things had indeed been hard.

Further encouraged by Raider's nod, Jethro continued. "Los Angeles wasn't no better for us. Buncha crooked gamblers cleaned us outta what little we had. We was hopin' that if we could make a stake outta holdin' up a stage, just one stage, we'd have enough money to head on back to where we come from, so's we could start over again."

"I think there'll be a little delay," Raider said, annoyed by the man's prattling. He did not like men who tried to solve their problems by shoving shotguns into other men's faces.

Any further talk was interrupted by a halloo from down the

trail. Standing in his stirrups, Raider saw Hume about two hundred yards away, at the head of a posse of a dozen men. He nudged his horse forward. The two groups met in the middle of a large clearing, where winter water had evaporated, leaving an open space. "I see you got 'em," Hume said, jerking his head in the direction of the two prisoners. "Did they say anything?"

Raider sensed where Hume was heading. "Nothin' that'd link 'em to organized robberies," he replied. "There was nothin' at all organized 'bout what they did. They're just a couple of down-and-out drifters from Los Angeles."

Hume grimaced. "Like a hundred others. A real sinkhole, Los Angeles. Full of vagrants, gamblers, and fugitives from more civilized places. The worst elements from Sonora and the U.S. have been holing up there for years. If we could clean up Los Angeles, it would go a long way toward establishing law and order in this part of the state."

"Is it that bad?" Raider asked.

"Yep. That bad. It wasn't like that back in the fifties, but during the war the place was crawling with secessionist sympathizers. Of course, not many of them had the guts to head east and join in the fighting. It's been downhill ever since."

Raider said nothing, although he felt a tug of annoyance. Being a country boy from Arkansas, he felt sympathy toward the Southern cause, although he'd been too young to fight. Still, he knew the kind of man Hume was describing, ignorant men from the South, and Texas, and the border states, who would spend the rest of their lives blaming their bad behavior on the war. He'd heard stories about Los Angeles, about the numerous casual killings, the governmental corruption.

"Los Angeles is run by a mob of vagrants," Hume continued. "They elect the sheriffs, the prosecuting attorneys, the mayors, and judges. An honest man is out of luck in Los Angeles, unless he's tough as nails."

"Any chance these robberies are bein' planned down that way?"

Hume hesitated. "I doubt it," he finally said, rubbing his

chin. "I thought about it for a while, but Los Angeles is too damned far away. Hell, it's a twelve-hour stage ride. Too difficult to plan the kind of split-second robberies we've had to deal with. No. They're being planned a hell of a lot closer."

Hume fell silent. They rode on, Hume and Raider following a little behind the others. Lige and Jethro were slumped in their saddles, closely guarded by the posse members, most of whom were laughing and joking boisterously, as if they were the ones who'd hunted down and caught such dangerous prey.

Eventually they reached the area of the railroad. Raider looked at the shining rails, the raw scars of roadbed cuts against the mountainside. He felt a moment's resentment. He knew his feelings were irrational; stopping the railroads would be like stopping the wind. But he still didn't like it; the railroad, the final conqueror of the West, the old West that Raider had more or less grown up with, but which he realized was doomed—mostly because of those shiny iron rails. It had been remoteness, inaccessibility, that had made the old West what it was. Now, any Eastern tenderfoot could buy a train ticket and be all the way to California in days, a journey that, just a few years earlier, had taken months. They would flood in, the two-bit farmers with their wasted, scrawny wives and their hordes of snot-nosed brats, until a man wouldn't be able to find an ounce of solitude.

Hume appeared to be having similar thoughts, but with different conclusions. Motioning toward the rails, he said, "That's the kind of thing that'll clean up places like Los Angeles. So far, those bastards have been off in their own little world. But the railroad will bring the world to them. It'll bring in good, honest people, and when they're in the majority, they'll insist that the law be obeyed, that killers and thieves be swept off the streets."

He turned toward Raider. "I know you don't care much for the Big Four, but, even with all their greed and arrogance, they're civilizers. They brought us the railroad."

Raider nodded curtly. The Big Four. Huntington, Crocker,

Stanford, Hopkins. Four men, former store owners, who'd had the undeniable guts to put together a plan to bring the rails over the incredible mountain ranges that cut California off from the rest of the nation. It had taken unbelievable drive and energy to pull it off, but that drive and energy had been accompanied by a mountain of ego, greed, and arrogance. Having brought California kicking and screaming into the nineteenth century, the Big Four had begun to believe that what was good for them must be good for California. To make their rail lines paramount, they had cheated and gouged, and even killed.

Land had been one of their foremost weapons. During the building of their Central Pacific line, they'd pressured the federal government out of huge tracts of free land. They'd leased that land off to farmers, first letting them move onto the land with the option of improving it, then buying full title later at a specified price. But they had reneged on their promises, letting the farmers and ranchers put their lives and hearts into empty, wild land, and then, when it had been tamed, the railroad had arbitrarily changed the purchase price, raising it so high that an ordinary farmer could not afford it, so that they were forced off the land which they had improved and made valuable, land which now went back to the newly-formed Southern Pacific Railroad Company, to enrich the Big Four. And if the farmers resisted eviction, there were always railroad gunmen ready to force them off. Or to kill them if they resisted.

"Yeah," Raider finally replied. "They done one hell of a lot for California."

CHAPTER THREE

When Raider, Hume, and the posse got back to Caliente, the prisoners were turned over to the local law. The posse members repaired to the nearest saloon to relive their adventures, while Hume and Raider returned to Hume's office inside the Wells Fargo building. As the two men once again seated themselves in the chairs they had vacated three hours earlier, when news of the stagecoach robbery had burst in from the street, Hume looked at Raider appraisingly. "The reports were right," he finally said. "You do good work."

"Thanks," Raider replied with appropriate modesty. But he felt good. Coming from a man like Hume, that was a real compliment. "But I s'pose it won't get us a gnat's ass closer to solvin' the real problem—them organized robberies you was speakin' of."

Hume shook his head. "Not even a little bit. Amateur road agents like the two you nabbed today are flea bites compared to the losses we've been taking from the gangs."

"We? Who's we?"

"I'm using the word in the general sense. My particular concern, Wells Fargo, handles the stage traffic between the railroad and southern California, plus other routes here and there. We transfer money, goods, and people, and we're getting hit hard. The people who are paying your freight, the railroads, are losing payrolls, supplies, and sometimes men. Regularly. All you've seen so far is the mess those two amateurs made of their robbery. That's not the way it goes with the gangs. They don't end up with five dollars taken from somebody's private letter. Every time they hit us they get their thieving hands on at least several thousand dollars. They seem to know just when the more valuable shipments are going to go out, or when a traveler is going to be carrying lots of cash.''

''Then there must be a leak somewhere.''

Hume shrugged. ''Probably. That's the first thing I thought of. But where? I followed every possible lead inside Wells Fargo—shipping agents, drivers, clerks—and came up with absolutely nothing. Which didn't surprise me. Many different types of targets are being hit, with more than half of them having nothing to do with Wells Fargo shipments. A source inside the company could not possibly be responsible for all the robberies.''

''Inside the railroad organization, then.''

Hume shook his head. ''Once again, we run up against the same problem: too broad an area of trouble.''

Raider scratched his chin. ''The more I hear, the more it sounds like the same kinda trouble I was investigatin' up in the San Luis Obispo area. Very professional robberies, with only targets carryin' lots of money bein' hit—as if someone was tippin' off the gangs. I wonder if there's a connection—''

Hume shook his head vigorously. ''I doubt it. There's too much distance involved, and not only distance, but terrain. There's some damned rugged mountains between here and the area you're talking about. I don't see how there could be any coordination. No, probably just two groups with the same idea. Whatever that idea is.''

Raider made no reply, just stared down at the floor, but privately he was not completely convinced by Hume's logic, although it sounded sensible enough. San Luis Obispo was almost three hundred miles away, separated from this part of the state by the Sierra Madre range, a wild stretch of mountains that, in some areas, was nearly impenetrable. How could anyone coordinate robberies over such a distance? Still, the similarities—

"Why don't we set a trap?" he asked Hume.

"Trap?"

"Sure. Spread word around that a real rich shipment's goin' out, then bushwack whoever hits that phony shipment—if they do hit it."

Hume nodded slowly. "Hmmm—I suppose—"

"Maybe we can catch us some live road agents. And maybe they can tell us where they get their information—if that's the way they actually operate."

"It's got to be!" Hume said forcefully. "I like your idea, Raider. I'll start figuring a way to spread around some false information about a big gold shipment that doesn't actually exist—"

Raider could see that Hume was already lost in the planning. Nothing much for him to do for the moment. "Is there a hotel in town, some place where I can stay a few days?" he asked.

"Huh?" Hume, absorbed in his thoughts, looked up at Raider somewhat distractedly.

"Some place I can hang my hat," Raider prompted.

"Oh, sure. There's more or less a hotel not far from the office. I'll have the clerk outside take you over there—introduce you—"

"No thanks. I think I'll just kinda keep outta sight for a while, try not t' connect myself t' your office any more'n I already have, which has been way too much. Then, when we're ready t' spring the trap—"

Five minutes later Raider was riding down Caliente's main street, toward the rather unprepossessing hotel to which Hume had referred him. It was a weathered frame building three stories high, boxlike in construction. Raider took a room on the second floor, near the back, in a corner over a narrow alley. The room's single window was set fairly high in a blank wall. It would not be easy for anyone to climb into the room from outside, but the window was low enough so that Raider could drop to the ground if he needed a quick way out. When he checked in, the clerk paid no attention to him at all.

Once he'd hauled his gear upstairs, Raider took his horse to the local livery stable and made certain that the animal would be well cared for. It was now time to care for himself. There was a public bathhouse down the street. After returning to his room for a change of clothes, Raider headed for the bathhouse. Ten minutes later, with his gunbelt hanging within easy reach, he was luxuriating in a tub of relatively hot water. He watched the water take on a light tea color as the dust soaked off his skin. He ordered a clean tub of water, and let himself soak for a half hour more, cooking the stiffness out of muscles that had been too long in the saddle.

Clean, relaxed, and in fresh clothing, he sought out a restaurant. There were a few greasy spoons with the usual meat, potatoes, and gravy, but Raider chose a small place run by a Mexican family. That was one of the best features of working in the Southwest—the availability of Mexican food. It was the kind of thing that grew on a man, an irrational craving, an addiction, this love of chili peppers and tamales, of meat stewed in sauces so spicy they'd probably take the paint off a locomotive. Raider sighed as he forked down a plateful of enchiladas. Sweat streamed off his brow. My God, the cook sure as hell knew his chilies! Occasionally, Raider took a sip of cold beer to cool the fire a little. The effervescence of the beer contrasted perfectly with the bite of the chilies.

As he ate, he allowed himself a little personal reflection. Here he was, in another godforsaken hole, staying in a fleabag hotel, about to risk his neck protecting somebody else's money. Worse, protecting the money of men he despised: the robber barons who were raping the nation, squeezing the working man.

Well, not much he could do about it. That was the kind of work he did, work he'd done for so long he couldn't imagine doing anything else. He didn't have a fancy title like

Hume. He was just an operative, one of hundreds—well, at his level, one of dozens—an operative of the Pinkerton National Detective Agency, the leading private police force in the United States. Maybe in the world. There was a certain amount of gratification in working for the best.

A month ago the head office had sent him to San Luis Obispo County, to investigate a rash of robberies that had been troubling the area. A few of those robberies had been against stage lines, but most had been against private individuals, travelers, ranchers in remote locations, even an occasional country inn or general store; smaller people, none of whom could compete with the railroads for the agency's attention. The railroads were rich. They regularly paid the agency one hell of a big annual retainer for its protection.

So Raider had been pulled off the San Luis Obispo robberies. He could imagine Alan Pinkerton sitting behind his immense desk in his cluttered Chicago office, either reading a railroad telegram, or maybe even speaking directly to one of the Big Four over that newfangled contraption, the telephone, licking his chops as he told Huntington, or Crocker, or one of them, just how much the agency's help was going to cost them. Not that Raider would see much of the money. Pinkerton operatives were notoriously poorly paid.

Raider didn't really mind. Hell, he couldn't believe that anybody was actually foolish enough to pay him for what he would have done for nothing. He loved his work. Even as a boy, he'd been a hunter, and now he was being paid to hunt that most dangerous of all game: man. Not just any kind of man, but the kind he detested. Men who robbed and killed, men who made victims of the innocent.

Of course, he didn't feel too comfortable backing up organizations like the railroads, or the stage lines, or the banks, but that's who paid the bills. Raider liked to think that the eventual winner was the common man, the real victim, the stagecoach guard or bank clerk or train engineer who was the one most likely to stop a bullet. The big fish only lost money, not their lives or their livelihood.

Well, the rich always got richer and the poor poorer;
Raider knew that, but he didn't waste too much time philoso-
phizing. He liked the work, the freedom of it, and this was
the kind of work you had to take where you found it. Besides,
thinking too damned much could get a man killed, could fog
his mind. No, he'd rest up a while, let Hume set up the trap,
then it would be time to reel in some road agents.

CHAPTER FOUR

Knowing he would have a few days in town, Raider decided to spend them profitably. With so much money passing through the railhead, the town was full of people wanting a part of that money; salesmen, whores, pickpockets, preachers, and gamblers.

Gambling attracted Raider. Everyone seemed to gamble, especially lawmen and politicians. Sheriffs, marshalls, deputies, judges, mayors, councilmen, tended to add to their income via games of chance. Of course, not all could win, but gambling brought together in one place the local power structure, brought them together in casinos, bars, and back rooms, where they could decide how best to fleece the electorate.

Raider was not a particularly brilliant gambler, but he played well enough. His specialty lay in holding his liquor. He always drank a considerable amount when he played, which led his opponents to believe that he was drunker than they were. He never won much, just enough to keep his opponents in the game, giving them hope that they would be able to win at least part of their money back.

He quickly discovered that Caliente, as a railhead, had attracted some very adept gamblers. For two days he repaired to the saloons, choosing those with the highest-stakes card games, and for two days he was barely able to stay even.

By the third night he'd decided that his most formidable opponent was a smooth, well-dressed man named Depuy, who claimed he was from Saint Louis. Depuy played a quiet game, folding often. However, when he did bet, he usually won, betting shrewdly, never letting anyone bluff him, almost as if he already knew what cards his opponents held.

That particular night, Raider had been winning fairly steadily from most of the others at the table, but not as steadily as Depuy. He was certain that Depuy was cheating, had been certain since the night before, but he could not find out just how he was doing it. Raider had watched Depuy's sleeves, had checked the deck for markings, had watched Depuy's hands to see if he was palming cards. He saw nothing, no obvious maneuvers.

After an hour of play, Raider was ahead about twenty dollars, a considerable sum to a man of his limited means. Yet Depuy was winning big, having nearly cleaned out three of the other players. The night before it had been Raider who'd been a big loser, down fifty dollars. He remembered his growing irritation as he'd looked into Depuy's expressionless eyes, eyes that always seemed to be looking right through him.

It was then that Raider figured out how Depuy was cheating. Last night he'd been seated opposite Depuy. Tonight they were seated on the same side of the table. Last night Raider had lost, tonight he was ahead, while the men seated across the table from Depuy were losing heavily. The night before, there'd been the sensation of Depuy looking right through him, yet he'd hardly glanced in Raider's direction tonight.

At the moment, Depuy was betting heavily against two men on the far side of the table. They obviously had good hands, or thought they did, but as the size of the pot grew, their smug grins turned into worried grimaces. However, they were now in too far to back out.

Raider looked up, right into the eyes of a man who was

leaning against the bar about twenty or twenty-five feet away. The man immediately looked away. Raider did the same, looking idly down at his cards, which were spread facedown on the table in front of him. He'd dropped out; the game was seven-card stud, and after five cards he'd had nothing at all.

Raider looked up again, not straight at the man by the bar this time, but a little off to one side, just close enough so that he could observe him without being obvious about it.

A signaler! The man was a signaler! Raider swore at himself. He should have guessed. The son of a bitch must have incredible eyesight; he was posted far enough away so that no one would have suspected him of studying the cards of Depuy's opponents, but that was exactly what he was doing; spotting cards as each man studied his hand, then using some kind of code to let Depuy know what he was betting against. Raider watched the man by the bar run through a repertoire of grimaces, small hand movements, and shakes of the head, all without looking directly at Depuy.

The next round of betting was due. Raider glanced at Depuy out of the corner of his eyes. Depuy was staring intently at the man by the bar, as he'd been doing the night before, when Raider was sitting on the far side of the table, getting the impression that Depuy was looking straight through him.

Raider felt a flash of anger. He ought to drag this slippery bastard out into the street and pistol-whip him. But, on second thought, how much more fun it would be to simply wreck Depuy's game.

As the betting rose to a climax, Raider excused himself, left the table, and headed straight toward the man at the bar, making certain that he walked between him and Depuy. He could imagine Depuy craning his neck, trying to see around him.

By the time Raider reached the signaler, it was too late for Depuy's opponents; he heard Depuy raking in the pot. Of course, the man at the bar had seen Raider coming, and he'd had little doubt that Raider was coming to see him; Raider had made it quite obvious, fixing cold unfriendly eyes on the man as he approached.

He was a rather skinny, pallid individual, and he turned even more livid as Raider drew near. He started to turn away toward the bar and his nearly untouched drink, but he seemed unable to look away from Raider. "Around these parts," Raider said in a voice too low for anyone but the man at the bar to hear, "we shoot varmints who do what you're doin'."

The man turned away jerkily, couldn't pull it off, then spun back toward Raider. He started to speak, couldn't, swallowed hard once, then bleated, "I—I don't know what you're talkin' about."

"I'll give you five seconds to get out of this bar. In six seconds you'll be dead."

Many a much tougher man had looked into Raider's icy black eyes, and backed down. The signaler swallowed once more, then nearly ran from the room, right past the table where Depuy was still counting his money.

Raider walked back to the table. Depuy was doing his best to remain cool, but there were little white pinch marks around his nose and mouth; he'd seen Raider run his confederate out of the bar. Raider could see him inching his chair back a little, perhaps ready to make a run for it if Raider unmasked him.

Instead, Raider smiled straight at Depuy, sat down next to him, and asked, in a voice purposely made casual, "Who's deal?"

It was Depuy's deal. Raider kept a cold smile fixed on him as he dealt. Depuy tried to remain cool, but Raider noticed that his hands shook a little, and once he nearly dropped a card. No doubt Depuy's most fervent wish was to get up and get the hell out, but Raider's smile pinned him in place. It was that smile, and the uncertainty of what Raider planned to do, that made it impossible for Depuy to leave.

Without his signaler, and in constant fear of what Raider might do, Depuy played poorly. He bet when he should have folded, he bet into better hands. Within a half hour he had lost all of his night's winnings, plus part of his capital. The men across the table recouped most of their losings, while Raider found himself over a hundred and fifty dollars ahead. He wondered if Depuy was losing on purpose, hoping that if everybody got their money back, they would be less likely to listen to anything Raider might say.

But the other players had already grown suspicious; they were quite aware of how dramatically their luck had changed after Raider had left the table and said something to the stranger at the bar. They had also been aware of the interplay of tension between Raider and Depuy. When, at the end of the game, Raider said to Depuy, in a voice as cold as ice, that he hoped Depuy would be leaving town quite soon, their suspicions were further aroused, but before anyone could act, Depuy had already left the table and was on his way out the door. "What the hell's goin' on?" one of the other players demanded, staring straight at Raider.

"He had a spotter over by the bar," Raider replied casually.

A general snarl passed around the table. One grizzled old track foreman muttered, "Why, that son of a bitch! We oughta take him out an' nail his hide to a wall."

Raider shrugged, then grinned. "I think his wallet's hurtin' a lot more'n his hide ever could."

After a moment's hesitation, the others grinned back. "Hit 'em where it hurts," one man chuckled. Five minutes later, they were once again immersed in the rigors of poker.

When Raider left the saloon an hour later, he was painfully aware that he should have walked out right after Depuy. He'd dropped forty dollars to all those grinning faces. Well, he was still over a hundred dollars ahead, and he had some interesting ideas on ways to spend the money.

However, Raider's winnings almost ended up going back to Depuy. Streetlights did not play a large role in Caliente's night life, and when Raider left the saloon, he stepped into intense darkness. But sight was not Raider's only sense; a man who did not rely on all his senses working in unison did not last long in Raider's chosen profession. He heard, coming from behind and a little to one side, the rasp of a leather boot sole against the gritty wood of the sidewalk. Instinct told him to move to one side and back, so that the club aimed at his head went wide, hitting him a glancing blow on the shoulder instead.

Raider grunted from the impact, and his left shoulder went numb. Having little doubt who his attacker was, he knew there'd be two of them. When he turned, he saw Depuy's spotter behind him, club in hand, readying himself for another swing. But where was Depuy?

No time now to wonder. He forced himself to stand his ground as he watched the club come down toward his head. Only at the last moment did he move, stepping slightly to one side. The spotter, believing that the first blow had stunned Raider into immobility, had fallen victim to overconfidence, and now there was no way he could stop his downswing. Raider simply laid his right hand on the butt of the descending club and took it out of the spotter's hand. With the club now his, Raider backhanded it across the spotter's face. Blood and teeth flew, and when the spotter raised his hand to his battered mouth, Raider slapped a hard blow behind his ear. The spotter fell like a sack of oats.

Which left Depuy. He came running out of the darkness, a slim dagger in one hand. Raider danced out of the way of the gambler's first frenzied thrust. For a moment he was tempted to draw his pistol and put a bullet through Depuy's gut, but the past few days had been rather boring; it was time for a little fun. Raider reached across his body and drew his bowie.

The sight of the huge blade caused Depuy to fall back several steps. He might have run, except that his back was now pressed against the wall of the saloon. His face twisted with a mixture of fear and rage. He lunged at Raider, trying to slip his lighter blade beneath Raider's larger one. Raider parried easily, and while Depuy was off balance, he brought his bowie down hard against Depuy's knife. There was a ringing of steel against steel, and Depuy's blade broke. The gambler looked down rather stupidly at what was left of his weapon, little more than the handle and an inch or two of blade.

Depuy tried to step to one side. Raider cut him off, the big curved tip of his bowie pointed at Depuy's face. Depuy licked his lips. "You—you wouldn't kill an unarmed man, would you?" he rasped.

"No more'n you would, you back-stabbin', four-flushin' son of a bitch," Raider replied drily. Which was small comfort to Depuy.

By now the noise had alerted the men inside the saloon. Heads poked out through the swinging doors. "What the hell's goin' on?" a man asked. He was one of the men who'd been playing against Depuy.

"This tinhorn figgered he'd get his losin's back the easy way," Raider replied.

Light flooded into the street as the doors opened. One of the men looked at Depuy, who appeared to be trying to crawl into the woodwork of the saloon's front wall, like a cockroach. "Why, that son of a— First he cheats us, then he tries to rob us."

"We oughta string him up," another man called out. Depuy cringed. The man then pointed to where the fallen spotter lay. "Him too. Somebody get a rope."

Raider slipped his bowie back into its sheath. "The idea's kinda temptin', but he ain't worth a rope. Now, on the other hand, a little tarrin' and featherin' might suit Mr. Depuy just fine."

There was an immediate chorus of assent. A half dozen men poured out of the saloon and laid rough hands on Depuy. His confederate, who was beginning to recover consciousness, was treated likewise. As Raider walked away from the saloon, other men were already taking off in all directions, hunting up those homey items necessary for a successful tarring and feathering.

Raider rubbed his shoulder. It was beginning to stiffen.

Later it would be sore as hell. What he needed was a hot bath and soft fingers to rub away the hurt.

Why not? Tonight's card game had left him with a pocket full of money. And damn if he didn't know just the place to spend it.

CHAPTER FIVE

The railroad had brought into this rather isolated area a great many men without women. Naturally, the presence of so many single men, men with money in their pockets, and no place to spend it, had attracted the attention of that universal solace of lonely men, the professional whore.

There were several houses of prostitution in town, most of them rather grubby establishments, with aging or ugly prostitutes. These houses catered to the lower-paid workers. The better houses had been set up for those with money and taste. Patting his pocket, currently stuffed with money, Raider cheerfully headed for the best house in town. He liked whores. He liked the institution itself. He considered it one of the few honest transactions possible between men and women. He'd had his share of love affairs. Most had ended in pain or regret. There was no regret with a whore, you got what you paid for, and when the transaction was completed, a man was free to go, free to live his life unencumbered. Maybe when he got to be a little older, say about eighty, he'd consider a more permanent arrangement.

The building that was Raider's destination, like most of the buildings in Caliente, was not much to look at from the outside. However, as one means of justifying its high prices, the establishment had spent a good deal of money decorating the interior. There were Oriental carpets on the floors, glass chandeliers, heavy maroon drapes hiding dirty windows, and a great deal of massive, overstuffed furniture. Or so Raider had heard. This was the first time he'd had a big enough bankroll to see for himself.

A doorman met Raider at the entrance. Raider's clothing did not exactly proclaim affluence, but a dollar tip gained him immediate entry. A small antechamber had been built just inside the doorway. Two beefy individuals politely relieved Raider of his pistol and knife. Only then was he passed through into the house's reception area. Once inside, he was pleased to see that the descriptions he'd heard concerning the establishment's interior had not been exaggerated; it was a little like walking into a maroon womb.

A rather large but not unattractive woman met him as he entered the room. She was dressed expensively, with her hair piled on top of her head in the latest fashion. She had the appearance of a well-dressed matron, the head of some prosperous businessman's household, although Raider doubted that the average matron would show quite so much tit. The rich fabric of her gown had been cut very low, baring an amazing expanse of impressively solid, creamy-looking flesh. Raider was certain that he could see the upper edge of one pink nipple.

The woman smiled at him. "I'm Hazel," she said in a deep and throaty voice. "How may I help you?"

Raider was about to tell her just what she could do for him, but he had second thoughts. If this was the madame, what must the girls be like? "Well, ma'am," he said, cautiously rubbing his sore shoulder. "I sure could use a pair of soft, healin' hands."

"Let me see," Hazel said. Very matter-of-factly she unbuttoned the upper part of Raider's shirt, then bared his shoulder. "My, my," she said commiserately as she studied the darkening bruise. "This day hasn't treated you very kindly, has it?"

Raider shrugged. "Well, ma'am, in some ways no, in other ways yes."

Hazel was standing quite close. Raider was becoming intensely aware of the perfume of her, not an artificial perfume, but the sweet, heady scent of a clean, very feminine woman. She was tall enough so that her bosom was quite close; he could not help looking down into the deep cleavage between her breasts, and once again he thought, why not Hazel herself? By the pound, she was probably the best bargain he'd seen in a long time.

Hazel, however, had other ideas. She picked up a little brass hammer and used it to strike a little bronze bell. The sweet, rich resonance of the bronze was still reverberating when a door opened and a girl came into the room, a girl so beautiful that Raider immediately forgot Hazel. "Clarissa," Hazel said to the girl, "take this gentleman into the parlor and introduce him to some of your friends. He'll be needing personal attention." Her composure cracked just a little as she wrinkled her nose. "And perhaps a bath."

Raider felt a little stung by that, but only a little. It had been a long day, with a great deal of tension around the card table. He probably smelled like a goat. Which was one reason he was here. A nice long bath in the company of someone like Clarissa would not exactly be an ordeal. He was already certain that Clarissa was the one he wanted; no doubt Hazel, as a professional, had correctly divined his preferences. Maybe the way she rang that little bell involved some kind of code, some way of summoning a particular girl.

Clarissa led Raider into a room that held four other girls, and now he was not so sure. Each one was lovely in her own particular way. Clarissa herself had a mass of thick dark hair which flowed over her shoulders. She was just a little above average height, full-bodied, but not overweight. One of the other girls was tall, slender, and elegant. With her ascetic face and wispy blonde hair, she was perhaps a little less earthy than Clarissa. Two others could have passed for sisters; very pretty, in a quiet way.

But the fifth girl literally shone; her glow radiated from her bright, blonde, curly hair, from her laughing blue eyes, from her rosy pink skin. She was introduced to Raider as Melinda. Now Raider's choice became really difficult. Was it to be Melinda the sun, or Clarissa the moon? An almost impossible choice. And then it occurred to Raider that a choice might not be necessary; he'd won a real piss pot full of money. Why not be creative in spending it?

He became aware that Hazel had entered the room, and was looking at him speculatively. "Have you made your choice?" she asked.

Raider walked over to her, drew her aside. "What's the goin' price for two at a time?" he asked in an undertone.

Hazel's eyebrows rose. "That depends on which two."

"Clarissa and Melinda," Raider replied, aware that his voice sounded just a shade hoarse.

Again that speculative look in Hazel's eyes, as if she were sizing him up, both financially and physically. "One hundred dollars," she finally replied.

"Sold," Raider blurted, then immediately regretted his choice of words when he saw a slight frown mar Hazel's otherwise cool demeanor. He was relieved when she finally nodded. "Clarissa, Melinda," she said, turning toward the girls, "would you accompany this gentleman into the bathroom?"

The two girls looked a little surprised. Raider saw them exchange hesitant glances. Was there jealousy between them? Some kind of rivalry? Good, he hoped so, because he was going to make them work real hard for their hundred bucks.

Falling in on either side of Raider, Clarissa and Melinda led him down a hallway and into a large bathroom. The bathroom's floor was made of wide planks, a warmer surface than tile. A huge tiled tub was built into a platform against one wall. Raider noticed that the tub had already been filled. Steam rose from the water.

The girls immediately began undressing Raider. They were, of course, quite professional about it. Off came his shirt. Both girls, who up until now had been smiling but reserved, lost some of that reserve when they had uncovered Raider's well-muscled upper body. The last of the reserve disappeared in squeals of delight when they'd stripped off his pants. "Oh, my!" Melinda burst out breathlessly. Raider wondered for a moment if it was a display of professional enthusiasm. However, the rapt manner in which the girl was studying his lower body made him believe that she was quite serious.

Clarissa was more composed. "You get into the tub," she said calmly. "We'll wash you."

"Of course," Melinda giggled, "we'll have to take our clothes off too, so we won't get them all wet."

"I can handle that," Raider grinned, tingling with anticipation.

First, the bath. The water was hot. Raider flinched a little as he settled into the tub, helped by the two girls. He quickly became used to the water's heat, and felt his muscles relax. However, when the girls began to undress, he felt one particular muscle tensing.

What a contrast! Clarissa's skin had an almost olive color. Her thick, dark hair hung down over pointed, full breasts. She had long, lithe legs and a taut stomach, with a dark patch beneath it. On the other hand, Melinda was irrepressibly— bouncy, that was the right word—golden-haired, ivory-skinned, impossibly lush, with round swelling hips and heavy, swaying breasts. Raider was glad that he had not been forced to choose either one girl or the other. He'd been right to go whole hog.

When the girls were completely naked, they piled into the tub with Raider; it was a squeeze, but not at all an unpleasant one. The washing quickly changed into other activities, and within fifteen minutes Raider knew he'd already gotten his money's worth.

Yet the fun had only started. The girls helped him out of the tub, then toweled him off, with many subtle pressures from breasts and thighs. They then led him, naked, into a room which was filled nearly from wall to wall by an enormous bed.

For the next half hour the two naked girls lovingly massaged Raider's body, easing the aches, taking most of the soreness out of his bruised shoulder. Lying facedown, he only slowly became aware of the byplay going on above him, between the girls. Hearing a sharp intake of breath, he turned his head and saw Melinda gently kissing the pointed, swollen tip of Clarissa's right breast. The way Clarissa was pressing herself against Melinda finally explained to Raider the look he had seen pass between the two girls when Hazel had asked them both to accompany him. They were the kind of women who liked other women!

Many men would have been offended, disgusted. Not Raider. Rolling over onto his back, he pulled both girls down on top of him. They came to him willingly, enveloping him, and each other, in a wealth of soft, moist, feminine flesh. ''Let's play us some games,'' Raider growled.

Over the next two hours, Melinda and Clarissa proved to Raider that their physical affection for each other in no way diminished their desire for a man. After a seeming eternity of soft breasts, wet, shuddering thighs, gasps of pleasure, cries of ecstasy, whimpers of longing, of need, plus the wild responses of his own aroused body, Raider knew without a doubt that he'd made one of the great bargains of his life.

CHAPTER SIX

It was a hot, clear, desert morning. Even the distant mountains showed no signs of mist or coolness. Still, the mountains would be a relief after all this unalloyed flatness.

Raider led his horse into the barn. The barn was quite dilapidated; it had been chosen as the meeting place because of its remoteness rather than for its looks. Inside, it was packed with men and horses. Most were Wells Fargo men. Heavily armed men. Today was the day the trap was to be sprung.

Hume was standing with several of the Wells Fargo group. When he saw Raider enter the barn, he left the other men and walked over to him. "You ready?" he asked.

"Well, I ain't too ready for that springless contraption you call a coach, but I'm ready enough for a fight."

Hume looked concerned. "Maybe you'd rather ride with the men."

"Uh-uh. I'll ride in the stage. You're too well known as bein' a Wells Fargo man. They might shy off, smell a trap, if they find out you're in there. You follow with the men. They're used t' you, anyhow."

Hume thought a moment, then nodded. Raider noticed that he looked a little flushed, somewhat excited, which was out of character with his usual cool, professional manner. But why not? These damned robberies had been plaguing Hume for a long time. Perhaps today they'd break the gang that had been preying on the area—if it was only one gang.

Raider spent a moment looking over the men. His life would probably depend on them. He noticed that they were looking him over just as carefully. He gave a slight nod; they looked like damned good men to have backing him up, hard men, steady men, armed to the teeth. Apparently Wells Fargo was careful in its selection, or had it been Hume who'd made the final selection?

Hume cut into his thoughts. "Time to go. Stage's leaving in half an hour."

Raider nodded. "Watch out for my horse," he said. "He bites."

Hume almost smiled. "We bite back."

Raider grinned. "Not too hard, I hope. He's a damn good horse."

The time for joking was over. Toward the back of the barn there was a buckboard waiting, already hitched to a two-horse team. Raider and one of the other men walked to the buckboard and got in. Raider took the reins. "See you later," he said to Hume, then shook the reins and guided the horses and buckboard out of the barn. The others stayed inside.

During the ride into Caliente, the man with Raider said little, only that his name was Sam. Raider said even less. Neither he nor Sam was heavily armed; they were wearing only their pistols. They had taken care to dress like travelers, stage line travelers. Raider was even wearing a black vest under a light jacket. He wished he wasn't; the air was already growing hot, and the vest itched.

When they reached town, they turned the buckboard in at the livery stable, then walked over to the Wells Fargo office, each carrying a small gladstone traveling bag. Raider's bag was of heavy cloth, decorated with a floral pattern. He didn't like it.

The stage was already there. Fresh horses were being hitched into place. The old team, dusty and lathered, was being led away to the Wells Fargo stables. Wells Fargo employees were loading cargo on top of the stage, and quite a bit more inside. Two men, dressed more or less the same as Raider and Sam, were waiting, holding similar gladstones. Raider frowned. Too much uniformity; if anyone was watching, was on the lookout, these similarities might act as a warning of something not quite right, of a concerted action.

Finally it was time to board. Raider, Sam, and the two other men got inside. There was not a lot of room. Long, wrapped packages took up some of the seat space. Flat bulky packages were underfoot, on the floor. Raider tried to make himself comfortable, then felt the coach sway as the driver and guard climbed up on top.

He became aware of someone talking loudly outside. Two or three people. One was a woman. He stuck his head through the stage window. A man and a woman were arguing with the dispatcher. "But we can't wait for tomorrow's stage," the woman was half-shouting to the dispatcher. "We want to be—we must be in Los Angeles by tonight."

"There really isn't any room, ma'am," the dispatcher protested.

"Really?" she snapped back. "I saw only four men get in."

"But there's freight."

"Nonsense. Freight goes on top, or in the boot. These stages are made to hold six or eight. I'll bet there's plenty of room."

She started over toward the stage. Raider noticed that the man with her said very little, was patiently standing back out of the line of verbal fire, the way a man with a bossy wife learns to act for self-protection. For the thousandth time Raider congratulated himself that he had never married.

The woman walked right up to the window on Raider's side of the stage. They were face to face. "If you'll kindly move aside, sir—" she ordered.

" 'Fraid I can't, ma'am," he replied, with a hard glare.

For the first time her self-confidence seemed to waver. She

found herself caught up in Raider's unwavering black eyes. She managed to tear her gaze away and looked past him into the stage, only to find that the three other men inside looked only a shade less forbidding. She also saw the packages. "I—I suppose it really is a little crowded," she said lamely, although it would have been possible to fit her and her husband inside.

Raider nodded. "Real crowded, ma'am. Real uncomfortable for a twelve-hour ride."

The woman hurriedly walked back to her husband. Sensing his wife's loss of composure, he almost smiled at Raider. Raider did not smile back. He did not admire henpecked men.

A moment later the stage rocked again as the driver lashed out with a long whip. The crack of the leather poppers, exploding just above the ears of the horses, sounded loud inside the coach. As the horses obediently surged forward against their harness, the stage lurched into motion. Inside, Raider and the other three men fought for balance as the stage began to rock and sway, as only a stagecoach can.

Raider had never liked stages. A trip in a stage was a nightmare of discomfort, dirt, and boredom, usually with too many people packed for far too long inside what felt like a big dice box being shaken by a giant. Given the choice, Raider would rather travel by horseback, with the opportunity to dismount when he pleased, to rest when he wanted, and also to be able to appreciate one hell of a lot more of the scenery around him. However, the advantage of a stage was speed, and the ability to travel with a lot of baggage. Stages traveled on and on, sometimes day and night without interruption, changing drivers almost as often as horses. Fast, yes; but still a miserable way to travel.

Speaking of baggage, it was time to open the bundles that were piled inside the stage. They were now far enough out of town so that no one would be able to observe. "Let's see what they've given us, boys," Raider said to Sam and the two other men. They nodded, and began tearing the paper and cloth wrappings off the packages, the long ones first, which proved to hold several rifles, two per man, all lever-action Winchester repeaters.

The flat bundles were filled with revolvers and ammunition, once again, two per man. Raider immediately began loading his two rifles and two extra pistols, as did Sam and the others. Within minutes each of them was surrounded by a small arsenal.

Raider rapped on the stage's doors and walls. Solid as a tree. Hume had told him that this was a special coach, of extra heavy construction, heavy enough, he hoped, to stop bullets.

The four men sat in silence as the stage rolled over the flats. Within a half hour they had reached the first gentle grade up into the mountains. The pace slowed, making them a much more vulnerable target, but they traveled onward for another hour without incident. It would be nice, in a way, Raider mused, if the entire trip proved uneventful. He immediately shook off the notion. Today might be their one big chance to end this whole thing, to wipe out the worst of the robbers. Then he would be free to ride away from this desolate land. Perhaps he could head back toward San Luis Obispo, so that he could finish the job they'd pulled him away from.

He thought of Hume and his Wells Fargo men, following a half mile or so behind the stage. Or so he hoped, because if Hume and the dozen men with him did not show up when the going got rough, this stage, heavily-built or not, might prove to be a tomb for four men, himself included.

Another hour passed. Still nothing. He and Hume had devised various ways to disseminate the fiction that this particular stage was carrying a gold shipment to two of the largest banks in Los Angeles. The word had been going out for a week. If the bandits did have some system of learning about the movement of valuables, they should have learned about this phony gold shipment. But maybe they'd deduced that it was a fake. Maybe the man and woman back at the Wells Fargo office had been scouts. Maybe right at this moment they were warning the bandits of the four heavily-armed men inside the stage.

Not likely. They'd still been standing there when the stage pulled away. No. If there was going to be an ambush, it still lay ahead, with the men in that ambush not knowing that they themselves were to be ambushed.

Raider studied the country around him. The stage route passed through big canyons and narrow valleys. Most of the land was arid, except at low points, where water collected, sometimes only underground; but if there was enough moisture, plants grew, usually dense windbreaks of willow, cottonwood, scrub oak, and heavy brush. Brush thick enough to conceal a cavalry troop, or one hell of a big gang of stage robbers.

The way got steeper as they approached the top of one pass. Along this stretch, the trail had been blasted out of solid rock. It snaked left and right. As the going grew more difficult, the driver slowed the horses to a sedate walk. Alarm bells went off in Raider's head. If the bandits were as good as they were supposed to be, this is where they'd hit the stage.

He stuck his head a little way out of the window. A sharp bend in the trail lay ahead, where the route curved to the left around an enormous boulder. More boulders rose to the right of the trail, forming a jagged wall. To the left, the ground was bare for a few yards, then was lost in thick brush and scrub oak.

"Goddamn!" he heard the driver shout. The stage immediately jerked to a stop. Sticking his head out a little more, Raider saw that several large logs had been laid across the trail, just beyond where it started around the rock.

He immediately pulled his head back inside the stage. "This is it, boys," he warned the others. Hands flew to rifles. Raider's eyes never left the thick patch of brush and scrub oak to the left of the trail. Sure enough, there was now movement among the trees. Two men, each carrying a shotgun, came running toward the stage, which, of course, could not move. Raider saw other men covering them from among the scrub oaks.

"Throw down yer guns!" one of the bandits shouted up to the driver and guard.

"Like hell I will!" the guard shouted back.

Damn it! Raider thought angrily, the guard wasn't supposed to fight, he was supposed to jump off the far side of the stage at the first sign of serious trouble.

One of the bandits raised his shotgun toward the driver and guard. Raider rammed the barrel of one of his rifles out through the window and shot the man in the chest. A moment later the blast from the guard's shotgun hit the man too; he was flung backward onto the ground like a bloody rag.

Someone shouted from amidst the scrub oaks. A volley crashed out from that direction. Raider could see the muzzle flashes, could hear bullets smacking into the coach. Overhead, the guard cried out in pain. Out of the corner of his eye, Raider saw him hit the ground behind the stage, near the big rock. The driver was down on the ground, too, but he didn't appear to be hit; he had displayed more sense than the guard, and at the first sign of shooting had scrambled down from his precariously open perch.

By now both Raider and one of the other men had their rifles poking out of the window and were blazing away at the brush and oaks. The problem was, the two of them and their rifles nearly filled the window; two rifles were all they could bring to bear.

Raider pulled away from the window and motioned one of the others to take his place. "Two men inside, two outside," he snapped. He and Sam backed out of the stage, then Sam ran to the front, where, crouching below the driver's box, he emptied a rifle, all twenty shots, into the oak grove.

The driver was bent over the guard. "How bad is he hit?" Raider asked.

"Shoulder," the driver replied laconically. "He'll live, the dumb son of a bitch."

Raider worked his way to the rear of the coach. To fire

without exposing too much of his body, he had to transfer his rifle to his left shoulder, but he was an equally fine shot either way.

So far, the unexpected heavy resistance had put a crimp in the bandits' plan. The men in the trees had obviously been put there to give fire support to the two shotgunners who'd rushed the stage. It had not worked out that way; the man Raider and the guard had shot was lying on his back, apparently dead; the other shotgun man had made it partially to cover, but now lay on his face, with at least two bullet holes in his back. He seemed to still be alive; he was making feeble crawling motions, but he wasn't going anywhere very fast.

Still, the only real ace in the hole Raider and the others had was Hume and his posse—if they showed up. Raider and his men were pinned down behind and inside the stage. The men in the grove would eventually be able to work their way to high ground, taking away the advantage of cover that Raider and his men now enjoyed. They'd either have to surrender, or be picked off one by one. Raider doubted that the bandits would break off the fight, they were boring in hard. Real professionals. Most bandits, hit with such a firestorm of resistance, would have simply pulled up stakes and ridden away.

Raider was reloading one of his rifles when Hume and his dozen men arrived. There was no hesitation; they rode in at a gallop, howling like Indians and firing their rifles from the saddle. They simply swept right around behind the oak grove, pinning the gunmen hidden there between two fires. One man, in fear of the horsemen pounding down on him from the rear, burst out of the oak grove, looking behind him. Sam immediately shot him down.

Carrying a rifle, with two extra pistols stuck into his belt, Raider left the cover of the stage and sprinted toward the oak grove. He could hear Sam, and maybe one more man, pounding along after him.

Raider ran in among the trees and brush, firing his Winchester from the hip. A man sprang up in front of him, tried to fire back, but Raider cut him down with three fast shots.

He heard scuffling to his left. He spun. One bandit, running through the trees and brush, had come up on his blind side. Sam shot him down even as the man was drawing a bead on Raider.

The two-sided attack, horsemen behind, Raider and two men from the front, had shattered the last of the bandits' resistance. Men were crying out in pain. One was sobbing like a child. "Hold your fire!" Raider shouted. "We wanna take some of 'em alive!"

Then he heard hoofbeats pounding away up the trail. It couldn't be any of the Wells Fargo men, they were all farther back; they couldn't have gotten around the grove yet. It had to be one of the bandits. "After him!" Raider shouted.

Two horsemen started in that direction, but were stopped by heavy rifle fire coming from a rock outcropping up near the trail. A Wells Fargo man fell, knocked out of his saddle by a bullet. The other one immediately pulled his horse around and raced back toward cover.

Raider saw Hume riding toward him through the brush. "We cleaned 'em all out, back there in the trees," Hume said. "What the hell's going on up ahead?"

"Some man with more guts than brains has holed hisself up in some rocks. He's sealin' off the trail, an' one o' the bandits is ridin' away safe as apple pie."

"We've got to get that man out of those rocks, then," Hume snapped testily. "I don't want even one of them to get away."

"Well, whoever's in those rocks ain't the kinda gent you just walk up on."

"Of course not."

Hume was in charge now, these were his men. After making certain that all the bandits in the grove were taken care of, either dead or held captive, he formed the bulk of his men into a firing line, with every one of them aiming at that patch of rocks.

The rocks were not very large; there was not all that much

cover. The gunman must be hugging the ground like a snake. "Open fire!" Hume shouted. A dozen rifles opened up on the rocks, every man firing until his rifle was empty. Dust boiled up from the ground, rock chips flew, bullets caromed from rock to rock.

After the first few rounds, not a shot came back from the rocks. As the firing died away, a man's voice called out weakly, "No more, boys, for God's sake, no more. I'm all shot to hell."

"Throw out your guns," Hume shouted back.

"Cain't." The voice was very weak. "Too bad hurt to move."

"Goddamn it, throw 'em out!" Hume repeated.

Raider laid a hand on his arm. "Just hold on a moment," he said gently. Then, holding his rifle ready, he began walking toward the rocks, watching carefully for a gun barrel to show itself. None did. He walked in among the rocks and found a man lying on his face in a pool of blood. The man tried to look up at Raider, but he could barely move his head. "Come on in," Raider shouted back to Hume. He knelt down next to the man.

"Turn me over on my back," the man said weakly. "I got dirt in my mouth."

Raider carefully turned the man over. The man's face whitened with pain, but he appeared to be grateful for a chance to look up at the sky instead of down at the earth. "Why didn't you run?" Raider asked. "The trail's right b'hind you."

The man swallowed. "A bullet had already busted up my leg real bad. Could hardly move. Decided to cover Theo while he rode on out."

"Theo?"

"Yeah—Theo."

The wounded man's attention seemed to waver for a moment. Raider knew he wasn't far from dying. He had, besides the shattered leg, several bullet holes in his chest and neck. Raider wondered how he was able to talk at all.

Hume came pushing his way among the rocks. "He's still alive?"

"Barely," Raider replied.

Hume knelt next to the man. "Looks like you're checking out, mister," he said with some gentleness. "Before you do, I'd like to ask a few questions."

The man looked at him blankly, then comprehension returned to his eyes. "Fire away," he half-whispered. He managed a faint smile. "But not the way you did a few minutes ago."

"How'd you know about this shipment?" Hume asked bluntly, knowing that, for this man, there was little time left for answering questions.

"Theo found out," the man gasped. "Went away for a day or so like he usually does, then came back with the news about all the gold. It was a trick, though, wasn't it? No gold—just men and guns."

"Yeah, a trick," Hume replied. "But the man who told this Theo about the gold—who is he?"

The wounded man started to shake his head, but pain stopped him, made him whiten again. Finally, he was able to reply. "Don't know," he said, in a voice so low that both Hume and Raider had to bend low to hear. "Only Theo knew. He and some other hard cases. They'd ride away from time to time, then come back a day or two later all hung over from bad liquor, but with whatever news there was. Except that this time the news was all bad—for us. For me."

"But you must know something," Hume insisted. "At least, what direction he rode. He—"

Raider laid a hand on Hume's arm. "Too late," he said softly. "He's gone."

And indeed, the man was dead. His open eyes were staring sightlessly at the sky above, the last thing he'd seen. A clear, cloudless sky. Raider nodded. A damned brave man, even if he was on the other side of the law. He'd deserved that last long look at the sky.

CHAPTER SEVEN

"I suspect that we spread the news around a little too broadly," Hume said morosely.

"With a shovel," Raider agreed.

"If we'd caught one of them alive, one who knew where the information about the gold shipment came from——"

"The one that got away."

Raider and Hume were seated in Hume's dingy little office. It had been nearly two weeks since the holdup and ambush. The immediate result had been a lot of dead and wounded bandits, but they were no closer to finding out who had been masterminding the operation than they'd been before they sprung their trap. And now, whoever it was had been forewarned.

"I figger we just shot up a lotta hired guns," Raider said, mostly to the wall.

"I figure you're right. And in an area like southern California, we only scratched the surface."

"You figger another gang'll get t'gether. Start all over again."

Hume nodded. "Too damned soon."

Raider sat up a little more alertly. "I wonder what's happenin' up north—if those robberies I was checkin' out are still goin' on."

Hume shrugged. "You're bound and determined to make a connection, aren't you?"

"Only if there is one."

"It would surprise the hell out of me."

Raider abruptly stood up. "I'm headin' over to the telegraph office."

Hume waited until he was almost out the door. "You're barking up the wrong tree, Raider. There's just too much distance involved. They'd never be able to coordinate it."

Raider turned, one hand on the door jamb. "Mebbe not. But it gives my simple Pinkerton mind somethin' t' work on."

The telegraph office was a half block away. It took Raider only a few minutes to word a telegram to the Chicago main office of the Pinkerton National Detective Agency. His request was simple: to have the office send him the latest information on the robberies he'd been investigating in the San Luis Obispo area. Sure, it was a long distance away. But so was Chicago, and here he was, dealing with Chicago as if it were just down the road. This was the nineteenth century, an age of science. Anything could happen.

But not today. It was two hours later in Chicago than here. They probably wouldn't answer before tomorrow. To pass the time, Raider repaired to his favorite saloon, and managed to pick up fifty dollars in a poker game. As he left the saloon, he was tempted to go over to Hazel's place and see what Clarissa and Melinda were up to. As if he didn't know. But, fifty dollars would buy only one or the other. An inhuman decision. It had to be the two of them together, or neither. He was just going to have to save up another fifty dollars. Damn, but they'd spoiled him.

It was ten o'clock at night, but on impulse, Raider wandered over to the telegraph office. A sleepy operator was slumped behind the desk, one ear half-cocked toward the telegraph key. He sat up straighter when Raider walked in, caught between annoyance at being disturbed, and gratitude for a little company. "Say," he said when he recognized

Raider. "A telegram came in for you just about half an hour ago. A real long one."

So someone had been working late in the Chicago office. Probably Wagner, the old man's right-hand man. He lived and breathed agency business.

The operator handed Raider two pages of telegram; it was a long one, all right. Cheap as they were, the agency didn't pinch pennies on telegrams. Only on operatives. Damned Scotch skinflints.

Raider quickly scanned the message. Very interesting. Up in the San Luis Obispo area the robberies had been continuing unabated until just about the time he and Hume had sprung their trap. Not a thing since.

Raider felt himself growing excited. Damn! Maybe it was just a coincidence, but he'd be a fool to write it off as one until he was sure. And there was no way to be sure without figuring out the entire picture. Then it wouldn't matter, it would all be over, one way or the other.

Raider paced back and forth inside the telegraph office, trying to think. Should he drop things here and ride north? Hard to decide. Hard to think clearly. He was aware of the telegraph operator looking at him curiously; having received it, the operator would know what was in the message, had no doubt connected it to some kind of law enforcement business. Raider could feel the man's curiosity prying into his thoughts. Pretty soon he'd start asking annoying questions.

Raider abruptly turned and went out into the street. But thinking was no easier there. Too many distractions. Three drunken track layers staggered by, bawling loud, discordant songs. Hazel's place just down the street was pulling on him like a magnet, assaulting his mind with images of full breasts and soft thighs. Even Hume, a damned good man, but a man with another mind, a man with different theories, was beginning to bother him.

Time to get out of Caliente, head for open, wild land, where a man would be bothered only by the wind and the sun and rain. Except that it didn't rain here in southern California in the summertime.

No point in heading north. There had been nothing to find there earlier, probably less to find now. Something, perhaps instinct, perhaps some bit of information which he'd not yet quite digested, suggested to him that this area was the center, that the root of the problem lay here in the southern part of the state. If that was the case, he might as well spend his time in the open down here. He could both do some thinking, and also do a little reconnoitering. It was time he grew more familiar with the terrain. A man could not work in ignorance.

He only slept a few hours that night. He was up before dawn, ready for the trail, bedroll and saddlebags in place, both rifles in their saddle scabbards. His horse, after nearly two weeks of inactivity, was raring to go.

He'd already written a note to Hume. He slipped it underneath the closed office door, then rode out of town just as the first of the track crews were beginning to shuffle out of their barracks.

He headed straight down the stage and wagon road that led toward Los Angeles. By sunup he had reached the place where the two amateur stagecoach robbers, Jethro and Lige, had come to grief. He rode straight on past.

He hesitated a little longer when he reached the site of the ambush. Men had died here, quite a few of the bandits, and one Wells Fargo man. Raider glanced over at the pile of rocks where the man with the smashed leg had breathed his last, looking up at the sky.

Raider pushed on. It was rugged, arid, harsh country. He rode through dry washes and up rocky canyons. He rode at as steady a pace as his horse could stand, stopping to rest only every three or four hours. He rode without thinking, letting his mind clear, letting it sweep itself clean.

He was over the Tehachapis by early afternoon. On the other side of the mountains, he found more flat desert. High mountains lay ahead, a southern branch of the Sierra Madre range. Late in the afternoon he started up a steep, punishing grade. He knew, after the long day's ride, that it would be hard on his horse, but he wanted to toughen the animal.

But not kill it. By an hour before dark he had reached high country again, this time a little greener and more pleasing to the eye. The higher elevations were well covered in pine, with pleasant oak groves a little farther down. He rode up into the pines, where, in a small mountain meadow, he shot a rabbit. He made camp only a few hundred yards from where he'd shot the rabbit, near a small stream that bubbled down from a spring near the summit.

He'd left Caliente too quickly to outfit himself with much food. The rabbit was appreciated, was his entire meal, except for a little hardtack. He'd have to do better soon.

He had picked a spot about a mile off the main trail. As it grew dark, he was surrounded by an intense silence. Even the wind was stilled. In that small moment of time when the sounds of the day have stopped, and the night sounds have not yet begun, he lay in his bedroll and watched the starshine grow in strength above him. A little later a half-moon came out from behind a mountain peak and bathed the entire area in a silvery, quiet light. This sure beat Caliente all to hell. Beat any town. Maybe even beat Clarissa and Melinda. Well—maybe.

He was not aware of falling asleep, but was aware of half-waking several times during the night to check his surroundings. Nothing threatening. Once, the high, shrill cry of a rabbit about to become something's dinner; another time the hoot of an owl. The distant yipping of coyotes.

He started out early the next morning, aware that he was damned hungry. Gnawing some hardtack helped a little, but not much. By late morning he had passed a couple of small settlements, just a family or two trying to wring a living out of these high, rocky, mountain valleys. He did not stop, not yet choosing to endure the company of men.

A little after noon his hunger won out. He spotted a collection of buildings several hundred yards off the main trail. It looked like a busy, prosperous place. Sometimes it was less hassle to get in and out of a busy place than an isolated one. In the isolated place, lonely people were eager to talk. In the midst of a bustle of activity, it was easy to slip in and out almost unnoticed.

As he rode in among the buildings, he saw that a Wells Fargo stage was sitting next to the largest structure. There was a sign over the building's big front door, which read, "New South Wales Inn." It was a roadhouse, then. New South Wales. Strange name. Where had he heard that phrase before?

One of the smaller buildings appeared to be a general store. Avoiding the main structure, the roadhouse itself, Raider rode over to the store. He dismounted on the far side, screened from the roadhouse. He did not quite know why he was being so careful; he simply did it out of instinct.

He went inside. He was the only one in the store, other than a bored clerk. He bought some bacon, a few cans of beans, some coffee, and two cans of peaches. He'd shoot fresh meat along the trail.

The store had one small window set into a side wall. Through the window, Raider saw a tall, heavyset man walk out of the roadhouse's front door along with two other men, then head for the stagecoach parked out front. He recognized the two men; they worked for Wells Fargo. They must be the driver and guard for this particular stage. The big man had his arms draped over their shoulders. He was smiling, but Raider did not like his smile. It was too much like a cat's rigid grin when it already has its claws into the mouse.

He caught snatches of talk, but could make out only some of the words. Raider turned toward the store clerk, motioned him over to the window. "That man," he said. "The big one. He has a strange accent. Cain't quite place it."

The clerk looked out the window, shrugged. "Oh, hell. He's an Aussie. Australian. He owns this whole kit and caboodle. Name's Logan."

Raider nodded. Australian. Of course. New South Wales Inn. New South Wales was a state or something in Australia. That explained his confusion over the accent. At first he'd thought it might be an English accent, but there had been something different about it. Australian. He took another look at the big man. He was laughing and joking as the Wells Fargo driver and guard got up onto their high perch. There was still something unsettling about the man's smile. Raider wondered if he was a Sydney Duck. In the past, he'd had a lot of trouble with Sydney Ducks.

Probably just his inbred suspicion nagging at him again. The man seemed prosperous, respected; the guard and driver had treated him like an old friend. Still, Raider's instinct told him to avoid the man. Carrying his purchases, he slipped out of the store, then loaded his saddlebags. Mounting, he turned his horse back toward the main trail. As he came out from behind the store, he realized that the Australian, Logan, was still standing outside, although the stage had already left. Their eyes locked for just the briefest of moments, and then Raider broke the contact by riding into a small grove of scrub oak.

Hard eyes. Logan had hard eyes, with a lot of suspicion hidden beneath the surface affability. A dangerous man—unless he was making too much of a few seconds of eye contact, bolstered by an inbred suspicion of anyone with an Australian accent—no doubt an unfair suspicion.

Raider put Logan out of his mind, returned to enjoying his trip. He veered off to the right, paralleling the headwaters of a small stream. Within two hours the stream had grown in size, meandering through the valley it had cut. It was a fine valley; Raider liked the look of the land. The mountains around it were quite barren, but the valley floor, because of the stream, was enriched by thick stands of trees.

There was not a great deal of settlement here yet, just an occasional small farm. That would change. The soil was rich. Many farmers would come, would take advantage of the presence of good soil, matched with at least seasonal water. The valley would fill up, lose its natural beauty, become a thing of neat artificial squares, a thing of man.

Raider camped that night in a patch of willows and cane,

near the lower reaches of the river. He knew that the ocean was near; he could smell it. He made a leisurely camp, enjoying his beans and bacon and coffee. In the morning it was coffee and hardtack, enough to get him on the road again. Following the widening river, he reached the sea forty-five minutes later. There was a town to his right. Seeing a Mexican working a little patch of ground near the trail, Raider stopped to ask what town it was. "San Buenaventura, señor," the Mexican replied. "Named after the old mission."

The Mexican hesitated. "The gringos call it Ventura."

Raider thanked the man, then continued on. A mile or two farther along, he rode his horse onto the beach. The stallion shied a little at the crashing waves, but seemed to like the sand.

Raider headed to his left, riding close to the water. Eventually, the lie of the land forced him away from the beach, but it was always within sight or hearing. He liked the soothing sound of it, loved its clean, spicy smell. Maybe when he got too old to be on the move, he'd find some place like this, with a stretch of quiet beach, and settle down. If he lived that long. And even if he lived that long, the place'd probably be wall to wall with settlers by then.

Rugged mountains lay inland. The farther he rode, heading more or less southeast, the closer the mountains approached the coast, until he was riding along a narrow strip of land hemmed in by cliffs on one side and the surf on the other.

At one point the solid wall of cliffs was broken where a strong little creek ran down toward the sea. Raider hesitated. If he continued on, he knew that he would reach the huge Los Angeles plain. He had, as yet, no desire to go to Los Angeles. The canyon the creek had cut enticed him. He wanted to see what was up in those mountains.

The going was not easy, but the higher up the canyon he rode, the more interesting the country became. Finally, topping the crest of a pass, he found himself looking down on as lovely a stretch of country as he'd ever seen. Between the mountains were meadows and slopes clothed in rich grass, with many stands of oak, sycamore, and cottonwood. Small streams abounded. From his vantage point, he saw two small herds of deer, several hundred yards apart. An enticing prospect.

Raider rode down out of the pass. It was a hot day, but a refreshing breeze was blowing. He studied the land around him more carefully. He noticed that, under the surface lushness, the ground was relatively arid, like most of this part of southern California. Very delicate land. If men came here, started damming up those little streams, used the water for what men use water for, started plowing into the fragile soil, this area could be turned into a desert. He hoped that did not happen. He knew that it eventually would.

He had ridden only a couple of miles down from the pass when he saw three men standing next to a wagon. He started toward them, intending to ask what this place was called. However, as soon as he was spotted, the three men turned and stared at him with overt hostility. The one in the center, the one the other two were flanking with blatant obsequiousness, was a very large man, tall and broad. The closer Raider drew, the more he was aware of how large the man was. There was a brutality about his size, a brutal air about his every move. When Raider was about forty yards away, the big man called out loudly, in a heavily-accented voice. "Hah! You! What you do here?"

Raider stopped his horse about ten yards away. "Thought I'd stop t' ask the name o' this place."

The big man thrust his chest out and stood with his enormous arms hanging out loosely from his sides. "Hah! You would do better to ask who *I* am."

Raider shrugged. "Okay. Who are you?"

The man seemed to swell up even more. Red in the face with the effort of his machismo, he boomed out, "I am Leonis the Basque, King of Calabasas."

"Really?" Raider said, scratching his head. "I didn't know we had any kings here in America."

The big man scowled. "Maybe not in America. But here in Calabasas, yes. This is my land."

"And is that your cow?"

Raider pointed down at a dead cow that lay next to the wagon. There was a bullet hole in its side. Leonis seemed to swell up even larger. "Damn yes! Every cow here in Calabasas belong to me! Damn squatter thinks it's his. But Leonis shoot cow, almost shoot squatter, but he run too fast. So now I have meat to take home."

So, the old squatter versus land baron game. Although, in Raider's experience, a lot of big-time Western land owners had also started out as squatters, claiming government land. They'd just been more successful at it than the little squatters. This big ox, with his kingly talk, was annoying Raider, but for the moment he said nothing, just continued to sit his horse, observing.

One sideboard had been taken off the wagon. Apparently loudmouth, this Leonis, was going to put the steer in the wagon and take it home as if it were really his own. But Raider saw no ropes or tackle. It was going to be a tough job for three men to lift a thousand-pound steer into a wagon with a bed that high.

Raider was not about to offer his help. Nor was his help asked. Leonis turned away from him as if he no longer existed, and then, to Raider's amazement, bent down and began dragging the steer toward the wagon all by himself. One of the other men stepped forward as if to help, but a snarl from Leonis made him back off.

It took a while, but damned if the big Basque didn't manage to get all one thousand pounds of cow up into the wagon. Raider was impressed. Sweating profusely, Leonis turned to face him. "You still here?" he bellowed.

Of course, he'd been aware all the time that Raider was still there. Raider had little doubt that the display of strength had been for his benefit. This big ox had the mind of a child. A dangerous child. He seemed very annoyed that Raider showed no overt fear of him. Raider was considering his next move, when Leonis made one of his own, launching himself at Raider's horse with a speed that was amazing in such a large man.

Raider's horse shied at the unexpected attack, unsettling Raider long enough so that Leonis was able to grab hold of his leg and drag him out of the saddle. There was no way for Raider to resist; it felt as if a grizzly bear had him by the leg, so, instead of fighting Leonis's grip, he slipped right out of the saddle so quickly that Leonis, surprised by the lack of resistance, lost his balance and fell, at the same time losing his hold on Raider's leg.

Leonis sprang back up onto his feet, but not quite as quickly as Raider. Then Leonis, a braggart by nature, took time to open his big mouth. "Maybe *you* some kind of squatter!" he bellowed.

He launched himself at Raider, but by now Raider had planned his next move. He was standing very close to the wagon. A shiny new pick handle lay just behind the driver's seat. As Leonis rushed him, Raider grabbed the pick handle, stepped to one side, and when Leonis rushed past, unable to check his wild charge, Raider cracked him hard on the shins with the head of the pick handle.

Howling from the agony in his shins, Leonis bent over, grabbing at the pain. Raider raised the pick handle high overhead. "Okay, King of Calabasas," he said amusedly. "Time you got crowned."

Crack! The hard hickory of the pick handle's thick upper end whacked against Leonis's skull. Raider expected him to go down, but, eyes crazy with pain, Leonis managed to stay on his feet, shaking his massive head. "Damn," Raider muttered, somewhat alarmed. He brought the pick handle down again, this time right behind Leonis's right ear. Leonis stiffened, his eyes rolled crazily, then he pitched full length onto his face.

Raider was aware that the two other men were moving toward him. He threw the pick handle at them. They tried to duck, one howling as the pick handle banged against his forearms. By the time they recovered their balance, they found themselves staring down the big hole at the end of Raider's pistol barrel. "I'm kinda losin' my sense o' humor," he threatened. "Back off, or you'll be as dead as that cow."

The men, neither of whom was wearing a gun, did indeed quickly back away. Raider saw a rifle barrel poking out of the wagon. He picked up the rifle and threw it into some brush. "I'm ridin' on outta here," he said coldly. "Don't go near that rifle till I'm outta sight. Understood?"

He received sullen looks from both men. "I said," he repeated sharply, "do you understand?"

Both men slowly nodded. Raider holstered his pistol and walked over to his horse. He never took his eyes off the two men as he mounted. Leonis was still lying on his face, breathing with a heavy, snoring sound. Apparently the pick handle hadn't killed him.

Raider turned his horse and was about to ride away when one of the men spoke. "Mister, I don't know who the hell you think you are—"

Raider stopped, and turned to face the man. "That ain't none o' your business, pilgrim."

"Well, he is," the man said, pointing down toward Leonis's prostrate form. "If he ever catches up with you, mister, you're dead meat."

CHAPTER EIGHT

Leaving the King of Calabasas peacefully sleeping, guarded by his faithful retainers, Raider continued east and a little south. After a half hour's ride, he was surprised to see a small settlement ahead, a number of ramshackle buildings, obviously hastily built, with cattle pens and horse corrals nearby. It had all the makings of a small cattle operation, although it was unusual to see a cattle outfit so concentrated in one place.

Unless one considered Leonis the Basque. If these were some of the squatters he had railed about, then they probably needed to congregate together for protection.

Curious, Raider decided to ride on in. This was, after all, a reconnaissance operation. Perhaps Leonis was behind the robberies. Perhaps he could learn more about Leonis here.

As soon as Raider was spotted approaching, men with rifles began to take up positions behind ready-made barricades. Raider rode in among the buildings, covered by a dozen rifles. He stopped his horse in a small cleared area, making no move to dismount. He was very careful to keep his hands in plain view.

A couple of men came out to meet him. They were appropriately scraggy-looking, squatters to the core. They watched him with hard eyes. "What might you want, stranger?" one asked suspiciously.

"Is there a head honcho 'round here?" Raider asked back.

"We're all equal here, mister—" the man started to say, but his companion, who appeared to be a little more intelligent, broke in, "That'll be Banks," he said flatly. He turned, and shouted out, "Hey, Banks! Some gent here wants to see ya."

A door opened in one of the buildings—shacks, really— and a tall, thin man emerged, carrying a rifle. Everyone seemed to be either carrying a rifle, or with a rifle close by. The tall man walked close to Raider's horse, although not so close that he would not be able to use his rifle. "You lookin' for me, mister?" he said in a flat, drawling voice.

"Not by name. Just saw the place. Thought I'd ride on in an' see what it was all about. Beautiful land 'round here. I was wonderin' if anybody owned it."

"Hah!" Banks snorted. "Guess you could get some argument 'bout that. It's government land, but there's those in these parts who got the gall to say it's theirs, an' no one else's."

"Like Leonis the Basque?" Raider asked mildly.

The men around him suddenly stiffened. "You come from Leonis, mister?" one of them rasped out.

Raider smiled. "You might say that. Ran into him a few miles back. Last I saw of him he was asleep on the ground."

"Asleep?" Banks asked, obviously puzzled.

"He got fractious. I had to rap him over the head a couple o' times with a pick handle."

A long, disbelieving silence closed in around Raider. Finally a man asked, awestruck, "You tryin' to tell us that you laid out Leonis?"

Raider shrugged. "He didn't give me much choice. There's one real bad-tempered man."

The tension was broken when someone laughed. "You kin say that agin, stranger," the man bellowed. "Haw-haw—he says Leonis has a bad temper."

General smiles broke out. "Step down a spell, stranger,"

Banks said amiably. "We'd like to hear more about Leonis an' that pick handle."

Introductions were passed around. It was an amiable bunch that escorted Raider toward one of the larger of the buildings. It was still just a shack, but there was a table and several chairs inside. More importantly, Banks managed to produce a half-full bottle of whiskey from behind a ratty mattress. There were apparently no glasses; Banks took a swig straight from the bottle, wiped the neck, then passed the bottle to Raider. Raider took his swig, then passed the bottle on to the next man. Besides Raider and Banks, there were three other men seated around the table. Raider regretfully realized that the bottle would not last long.

Raider leisurely recounted the story of his run-in with Leonis, letting the men around the table pull the details from him bit by bit. It made a fine tale, and the men were alternately breathless and amused. "Seems like you folks are pretty int'rested in this Leonis character," Raider finally said.

Banks grimaced. "More than we'd like to be. You've seen the land around here. It's good land, beautiful land, and it's mostly empty. Fine land for runnin' cattle an' horses, an' maybe raisin' some table crops. There should be room enough for quite a few different families, but Leonis—he just lays claim to it all."

"Yeah," another man growled. "Ol' Leonis, he likes t' steal land. First he stole his wife's father's land. Huge spread over near the San Fernando mission. But even that much land weren't enough for Leonis. Greediest son of a bitch that ever drew breath."

"You look new 'round these parts," Banks cut in. "Guess you never heard the story. Leonis came to the Los Angeles area quite a while ago, from France, or Spain, somewhere up in some mountains called the Pee-Runnies, somethin' like that. He used to brag about how he was a big smuggler over there, how he started out as a sheepherder an' worked his way up. My guess is that they run him outta France. Probably killed somebody. He's one mean son of a bitch, cain't even read. Anyhow, he lit in Los Angeles some years ago, not a penny to his name. But he wanted money, an' there was two ways to get it quick an' easy: loan sharkin' an' marriage sharkin'. Well, Leonis, hell, he couldn't hardly count anyhow, so he didn't have much chance at loan sharkin'. So he tried the marriage route.''

"Wait, wait," Raider cut in. "I understand loan sharkin', but I—''

"Oh, but you ain't never seen loan sharkin' like in Los Angeles," one of the other men said. "Hell, that's the way a buncha no-good bums got all those Spanish land grants away from the Spanish people here after the Mexican War. There was this one Irishman, over from County Cork, who used ta charge twelve-and-a-half percent a day on small loans, five percent a month on big ones. Well, one time he lent some rich Mexican fifty bucks so's he'd have some cash for a night out on the town. Now, those old Mex land barons didn't know much 'bout money. Among 'em, if a man lent another man a few bucks, the polite thing was t' forget about it. Gentlemen didn't go 'round grubbin' money outta people. But this Irishman weren't no gentleman, not the way the Mexes figger a gentleman. He had a loan note drawed up all nice an' proper, an' within the year that poor Mex owned him five thousand dollars on the original fifty bucks. Now, this Irishman tried t' pass hisself off as a good guy, so he wrote up the loan again at five percent a month, an' it just kept on growin' an' growin'. A few years later that damned Irishman took forty thousand acres o' prime land off the Mexican, all nice an' legal.''

"But Leonis had other ideas," Banks interjected. "Like a lotta other no-goods, he figured it'd be even quicker t' marry into land, so he married the daughter of some ol' Mex rancher over near San Fernando. The ol' man had thousands of acres. Leonis just kinda took it over. Now, that land lies real near Calabasas, just the other side o' the hills, an' Leonis just kinda expanded this way, rode right on in an' started usin' the land, no title, nothin'.''

"Yeah," the other man said. "His title ain't no better'n ours."

Raider shrugged. "But I s'pose he's got lotsa hired guns that make his claim good a little bit better'n the next man's."

"Not just guns," Banks replied. "He uses the law. If someone tries to move in here, Leonis goes to the Los Angeles sheriff an' charges the man with breakin' some kinda law. Leonis is in real tight with the sheriff an' the judges over at Los Angeles. A lotta men who've been careless enough to piss off Leonis have ended up goin' t' jail on trumped-up charges. But it's gettin' better. They's some lawyers over Los Angeles way, like Major Bell, who'll speak up for the little man. That's why we figure we got a good chance o' settlin' in here."

"If Leonis don't kill us off first," one of the men added sourly.

Banks shook his head. "If he tries it, he just might end up bein' the one gets killed," he muttered.

His face brightened, and he looked up at Raider. "Say. You look like a man who can handle a gun. What say you settle down here, take up some land with us, an' when Leonis comes around t' run us off, you can put him t' sleep for good."

Raider shook his head. "I'm not the settlin' down kind o' man."

Banks sighed. "Didn't figure you were. But hell, you kin stay a day or two, maybe go out huntin' with me in the mornin'. We're low on fresh meat."

Raider agreed, and one of the other men, after considerable inner turmoil, informed the others that he had a bottle stashed in his shack. The party moved outside, the men drinking in the shade of a huge oak tree. Raider had to admit that this was indeed a lovely piece of land. A few hours later he watched the sun go down over the western hills. Everything between himself and those hills took on a purple hue. Or maybe it was the whiskey that was making everything look purple; it was pretty bad rotgut.

That night he slept in one of the shacks, with a man asleep
on the other side of the room, snoring like a giant ripsaw. He
would have much preferred riding up into the hills, and
sleeping under the stars, away from the stink of man, but he'd
decided to spend a day or two with Banks and his fellow
squatters. Who knew? They might even be behind some of
the robberies. He'd seen some damned desperate-looking men
among the shacks.

A third bottle of red-eye had magically turned up the night
before, a tribute to the importance of Leonis's humbling by
Raider, so it was a bleary-eyed group that came stumbling out
of their shacks the next morning. Several pots of coffee were
brewing over various outdoor fires; the coffee helped, but
Raider was still feeling a bit rocky as he and Banks prepared
to ride out and collect some deer meat. Raider was just
slipping his Sharps into its saddle scabbard when Banks
twisted away from him. "Somebody ridin' in hard," Banks
said. "Hard an' scared."

Raider later figured that it must have been Banks's continuing struggle against Leonis that had warned him of trouble
coming. And trouble it was. Less than a minute later a rider
came pounding in among the shacks, his horse lathered, his
face white. "He's comin'!" the man was shouting. "Comin'
with a whole fuckin' army!"

Banks ran over and seized the bridle of the man's horse.
"Slow down, Hank," he shouted. "Tell us what you saw."

"It's Leonis," Hank shouted back. "He's only a coupla
miles away, leadin' what looks like a thousand men, comin'
on fast. God damn! A whole army, comin' on like the hounds
o' Hell."

CHAPTER NINE

Banks's reaction was smooth, instantaneous, and obviously preplanned. "George, the bell," Banks said calmly to one of the men. A piece of iron, an old plowshare, was hanging by a rawhide cord from the porch of one of the shacks. Picking up a poker, George ran over to the shack and began banging on the hunk of iron. It's loud ringing brought squatters running from every direction, every man of them carrying at least one rifle. The men immediately fanned out behind the barricades Raider had noticed when he'd ridden in the day before. His respect for Banks rose several notches. He wondered if Banks had had military training. The barricades were well-placed, covering the main approach into the squatters' little valley. Anyone attacking would have to ride straight at the barricades.

Leonis's manner of attack was a great aid to the defenders. He came in the same way he'd attacked Raider, with a mad, headlong rush; no thought, no planning, no subtleties, a mirror image of the way the man thought and lived, a mixture of greed and fear, the greed overcoming the fear by blocking out any rationalities. Raider saw the cloud of dust first, a big cloud, rising on the far side of the little hills that screened off the valley. There probably were a hundred men on the way, to Banks's thirty or so. Raider was aware of Banks next to him, talking. "We got us maybe a minute or two left,"

Banks said coolly. "Might be a good idea to hunt us up some cover."

Raider nodded. Together, he and Banks moved behind one of the barricades. It looked strong; it was made of logs and earth, with loopholes built between the logs for firing.

A murmur of tension swept through the defenders as the first of the attackers swept in through the entrance to the valley. They came in a pell-mell rush, strung out in no particular order. Raider tried to pick out Leonis, but could not; then he saw him, way back in the pack, almost invisible in the dust. Was he hanging back on purpose, to save his hide? Or was it simply that he was so heavy that his horse was lagging behind?

Banks rapped out a sharp order, warning his men to hold their fire until the main body of the attackers had reached a particular point. Raider noticed, then, that out in the little plain in front of the settlement, stakes had been planted in the earth. The stakes were painted different colors; aiming stakes, each color representing a different range.

The first few riders passed the stake Banks had specified. He waited until the main body had reached that particular stake, then he shouted, "Fire!"

Thirty rifles roared almost together, then roared again, much more raggedly, as fresh rounds were jacked into smoking chambers. Sixty chunks of hot lead plowed into the pack racing toward the barricades. The effect was devastating; horses went down, men were blown out of saddles, other clutched at wounds. The attack was stopped in its tracks, with men milling about in confusion, and others, wounded, trying to drag themselves, or their horses, out of the line of fire.

However, two of the attackers made it past the barricades, riding in among the buildings. One shot at Raider, but missed. Raider fired back with his Winchester, shooting from the hip, knocking the man out of the saddle. Banks shot the other man.

The attackers, badly mauled by that first terrible volley, had fallen back behind a small ridge. The ridge was only a few feet high, but it gave them adequate cover, just enough so that they could fire back at the defenders in relative safety. Raider was surprised that Banks, in his preparations for defense, had not had the foresight to level that little ridge.

Oddly enough, Banks was smiling. "Perfect," Raider heard him murmur. Raider was still wondering what was perfect, while Banks quickly rounded up eight men. He waved five off toward the left, and kept the other three for himself. He looked over at Raider. "Want to come along?" he asked, grinning.

"Hell yes," Raider said. He wasn't sure what Banks was planning, but he had little doubt that it would be interesting.

It was. The five men who'd gone left disappeared up a little arroyo, which screened their advance from the attackers. Banks and Raider and the other three men slipped to the right, behind a gully that swung out in a big, concealed arc.

It was a perfect flanking movement. Neither group could be seen by Leonis's men. Within a few minutes both flanking groups were in position, five men behind and to the left of Leonis's position, five more on the right.

Banks, Raider, and the three other men slipped into place behind a dirt bank. They had a clear view of Leonis's men as they fired at the barricades. Banks raised up a little. Raider looked too, and saw a man wave from the far flank. The trap was closed. "Okay, boys," Banks said in a conversational tone. "Let 'em have it."

Ten rifles crashed out, pouring fire into Leonis's men, both from the right and from the left. The attackers milled about in confusion. Several more men went down. They still had a chance. They could have rushed the two small groups on their flanks; their greater numbers might have carried the day, but this unexpected attack had filled their minds with unreasoning fear. Men ran to their horses, jumped into their saddles, and went racing back toward the valley entrance. Some even threw away their weapons so that they might run more quickly.

Leonis stayed for another minute or two, screaming curses after his retreating men. Raider raised his rifle and fired. He smiled when he heard Leonis shout in anger and pain, then grab at the seat of his pants. Raider fired again, knocking the heel off one of Leonis's boots. Leonis went down, and by the time he'd gotten back on his feet, at least a smidgen of reasoning power had leaked into that simian brain. Limping badly, both from the missing boot heel and the bullet that had creased his ass, Leonis made it to his horse, mounted, and rode away, looking back over his shoulder at the settlement, shaking his fist, screaming curses.

Banks fired at Leonis but missed. He turned toward Raider, his expression rather sour. "You coulda killed the son of a bitch," he said accusingly, "but you didn't."

Raider chuckled. "Killin' him wouldn't o' been half as much fun."

Banks thought about it for a moment, then smiled. "Maybe," he said. "But I'd feel a hell of a lot better with that bastard dead."

They stayed in position for a while, until a distant, diminishing dust cloud convinced them that the danger was finally over. The walk back to the settlement was a slow one; the tension and fear had made most of the men very tired. There were some cheers when Banks returned, but they were muted cheers. Two of the squatters had been killed, three more wounded.

Later in the morning several heavily-armed men went out into the little plain, looking for wounded attackers. There were none alive, only bodies. Twenty-two of the attackers had lost their lives. There was no way to tell how many of those who'd ridden away had been wounded. From the blood trails, plenty. Raider doubted that Leonis would be able to hire any more men to attack the settlement. His losses had been too heavy. Word would spread.

The burying of the dead went on all day. The attackers were buried where they'd fallen. Large crosses were pounded into the soft earth covering their graves as a warning to others who might be foolish enough to try the same thing. It was a grim afternoon. Death humbles even the winners, so it was a solemn group that went to their beds that night.

The next morning Raider was ready to ride. Once again Banks tried to talk him into staying, but was not too surprised when, once again, Raider politely declined. "Got some chores t' finish," Raider said quietly.

One of the squatters wanted to ride out with him; he'd had enough of life bucking Leonis. "That big ape ain't gonna quit," the man, whose name was Frank, insisted. "He'll keep chippin' away at us till there ain't a man left."

Banks made no attempt to dissuade Frank. Privately, he told Raider that Frank was a chronic complainer and malingerer; he'd be glad to see him go.

There were a few other waverers who showed signs of wanting to ride out. Banks cheered them up by reminding them of how badly they'd beaten Leonis only the day before. "He'll stay away," Banks promised.

Raider and Frank rode out a few minutes later. There was no big show of saying good-bye, but it was not out of unfriendliness. They'd all been in a fight together, they all felt a bond. Words were not necessary.

Raider and Frank headed east, toward a high mountain pass. "I don't like goin' this way," Frank complained. He pointed toward the southeast. "Over there, down toward the flats, that's all Leonis's land. He could be lurkin' out there anywhere."

"Then ride back the other way," Raider said curtly. He was growing tired of Frank's constant grousing. It had been an eventful couple of days: first, cold-cocking Leonis with the pick handle, afterward, drinking all that rotgut with Banks and the others, and finally, ending up in the middle of a full-scale war, with bullets flying thicker than lice on a chicken. Raider would have preferred being alone with his thoughts, to hearing Frank's annoying whine.

As he rode, he mulled things over. So far he hadn't found out any specific information that would point to whoever was behind the robberies he was investigating. However, he had learned a few things: first, the lay of the land, second, its general lawlessness. The fight between Leonis and the squatters had taken place only about forty miles from the Los Angeles County courthouse. A large number of men had been killed. The peace had been broken. Yet Banks had insisted that nothing would come of it, that it would simply be swept under the rug. Nobody wanted to mix in anybody else's dangerous business, unless it was for a profit. Apparently the local law was worse than useless—once again, unless you had the hard cash to buy it.

Banks had told Raider an anecdote about a visitor to the Los Angeles area who had been robbed by two men while riding through Sepulveda Pass, only a few miles from Los Angeles. When he had gone to the courthouse to file a complaint, he had recognized both the judge and the prosecutor as the men who'd robbed him. He'd been foolish enough to say as much. Banks claimed that the man had been lucky to get out of Los Angeles alive.

But back to the problem at hand. Detective work. What he needed was more detective work. There must be some common factor among all the details of the various robberies that would lead him in the right direction. The question was, where to look for it. Probably the best approach would be to get back to Caliente. Together, he and Hume, using the resources of both the Pinkerton National Detective Agency, and Wells Fargo, ought to be able to come up with some kind of pattern.

Raider suddenly stopped thinking. Something was wrong. It was quiet, too damned quiet. For a moment he thought that the quiet was due to Frank; having received no replies from Raider, he'd stopped yammering. No; it was more than that. The birds, the small animals, even the wind seemed to have fallen silent, as if something had disturbed the entire area.

"Get off the trail!" Raider shouted to Frank, at the same time pulling his horse to the side.

"Hey, what the hell?" Frank whined. "I ain't said nothin' that would make a fella—"

Kawoom! The roar of a large-caliber rifle drowned out Frank's voice, but did not quite overwhelm the meaty smack of the bullet that slammed into Frank's back. Frank literally flew out of his saddle. He hit the ground hard, then rolled over several times.

Kablam! The roar of a second rifle followed a moment later, its voice slightly different than the first. But this bullet missed, passing through the spot where Raider had been riding only a moment before he'd pulled his horse to the side.

Raider raced his horse toward cover behind a clump of trees. Kawoom! Kablam! The rifles roared again. Their heavy bullets clipped small limbs from trees, but both slugs missed Raider.

There were two rifles, firing almost together, which meant at least two men. Peering from behind one of the thicker tree trunks, Raider was able to see gunsmoke gathered in a growing cloud over a little rise of ground about a hundred yards away. Common sense said to ride out of here as fast as possible, but Raider had no intention of leaving Frank, whining voice or not, lying shot, maybe still alive, on the trail.

Two rifles, and from the sound of them, each one of a heavy caliber. Which almost certainly meant single shot rifles. Rifles that had to be reloaded each time they were fired.

The rifles bellowed again. One bullet broke a fair-sized limb in half. Damned heavy calibers all right, but even before the echoes of the shots had died away, Raider had broken cover, and was racing his horse from the cover of the trees, angling to the front, and a little toward his right. Timing would be everything; he had to make the cover of a pile of boulders before the riflemen completed their reloading—if there were indeed only two rifles.

He rode in behind the boulders only an instant before both rifles roared again. The bullets spanged loudly against the boulders. Rock chips stung Raider's face and hands, but he was already riding out from behind the boulders, looping around behind the little rise. He could hear the sharp click of the rifles' actions being opened. He could visualize fresh shells being shoved into the big chambers.

But Raider was already behind the rise, his Winchester was in his hands, and he was standing in the stirrups, guiding his horse with his knees toward two frantically busy men. Raider fired from the shoulder, sending bullet after bullet toward the two men. One of the men actually got his rifle to his shoulder and snapped off a shot, but the shot missed; Raider had already put a bullet through the man's neck, ruining his aim. Another of Raider's bullets tore into the man's chest, while two more bullets nearly took the head off his companion.

Raider swung down from his horse while the animal was still moving. Catching his balance, he let his momentum carry him right in among the two gunmen. He saw, immediately, that there would be no more fighting; the man who'd been hit in the head was obviously dead. The other man was so badly hit that he would soon join his companion.

Raider walked over to the wounded man, careful to kick his rifle several yards away. The man did not appear to have a pistol. Blood pumped from his chest and neck as he turned to look up at Raider. "Gawd, mister—" he moaned. "You done gone an' killed me."

Raider pointed the muzzle of his rifle at the man's face. The man shuddered and looked away. When no shot came, he dared look back. "What the hell was all that about?" Raider demanded.

"Wh-what?" the man mumbled. Blood was running from his mouth, making it difficult for him to speak.

"The shootin'," Raider snapped. "Why the hell'd you open up on us?"

The man did not answer immediately, but the fear had faded from his eyes. Perhaps he understood that he was going to die, that it was only a matter of minutes before his wounds killed him. Nothing could matter any more. "Money," he muttered.

"Money?" Raider replied. "What the hell d' you mean? Were you plannin' on robbin' us?"

The man tried to shake his head, but the pain of his neck wound made him cry out. He held his head very still, then tried to talk, but he began to choke on his own blood. Raider thought he had lost him, but the man, summoning up the last of his strength, managed to murmur, "Leonis—he paid us. Said—no more head-on attacks. He swore he'd get those damned squatters off his land by bushwhackin' 'em, one by one. But—"

The man began to struggle again, and this time he did not recover. One last big bubble of blood welled up from his mouth, and he died.

Raider left the two men where they'd fallen. Leonis had bought them, Leonis could bury them. Remounting his horse, he rode over to where Frank had fallen. He was as dead as the two bushwhackers. There was a neat round hole in his back where the bullet had gone in, and another hole the size of a dinner plate in his side, where the bullet had come out.

Raider was wondering if he should bury Frank here, or take him back to Banks's settlement, when he heard the sound of someone riding hard toward him. At least two men. More bushwhackers? Spurring his horse, Raider headed toward the trees again. He was well concealed when two men came riding hard over a hilltop. When they spotted Frank's body, lying in the center of the trail, they pulled their horses to a sliding stop. "Damn!" one of them cried out. "It's Frank!"

"Well, hell, where's that gent he rode out with?"

His companion looked around nervously. "Maybe lyin' dead somewhere, too."

"He wouldn't o' shot Frank hisself, would he?" the first man asked.

By now Raider had recognized the men as two of Banks's squatters. "Over here," he called out, careful to remain hidden in case the men reacted before they thought, maybe sending some lead his way. "Two men bushwhacked us. They got Frank right off, but then I got 'em. They're lyin' dead up behind that ridge off to your left."

"God damn!" one of the men bleated. "You scared

the hell outta me. Come on out where we can see ya.''

Raider rode out carefully, still holding his Winchester. The two squatters looked at him with great nervousness, so he suggested that they ride up over the rise and look for themselves. Only one made the trip. He came back down the hill a few minutes later, his expression grim. ''They're there, all right.''

He looked at Raider. ''You say they just opened up on you?''

''I didn't, but that's what they did. One of 'em lived long enough t' tell me that they'd been paid by Leonis. Seems like, since he can't take Banks head-on, his new plan is to bushwhack you squatters, one by one. You boys ride on back to Banks. Warn him.''

The men nodded. When they seemed about to turn their horses and head back the way they'd come, Raider pointed down toward Frank's body. ''And take him with you.''

The two men rather reluctantly rounded up Frank's horse, slung his body over the saddle, and were ready to ride within minutes. ''You sure you ain't comin' along with us?'' one asked Raider.

Raider shook his head. ''Naw. I figger I seen enough of Calabasas. It's real beautiful country, but I think I'll leave it to men like Banks and Leonis. They're willin' t' bleed for it. I'm not.''

CHAPTER TEN

"I should've made the connection right away," Raider said morosely.

"Why should you have?" Hume replied. "Even now, it's only a supposition."

"No. I know he's the one."

Hume scratched his head. "Then it sure knocks the hell out of your theory that our local robberies, and the ones near San Luis Obispo, are connected."

Raider shook his head angrily. "Mebbe. Mebbe not. But I do know that Logan is our man. Call it a gut feelin'."

It was actually quite a lot more than a gut feeling. It was the result of two weeks of intensive detective work. Using both the huge rogues' gallery of the Pinkerton National Detective Agency, and the resources of the Wells Fargo company, a solid picture had begun to emerge. First, operatives had tracked down most of the men who'd been robbed, looking for some factor common to all the robberies. That common factor had turned out to be the New South Wales Inn. And Logan. Most of the people who'd been robbed had either spent the night at the inn, had passed through on the stage, or someone who knew their movements had some other connection with the inn.

Which had focused considerable attention on Harold Logan,

the proprietor of the New South Wales Inn. There had been a considerable stack of information on Logan in the files of both the Pinkerton National Detective Agency and Wells Fargo. It was old information, long buried, but now that it had been unearthed, it made fascinating reading. ''I knew it!'' Raider had exploded when he received the agency report on Logan. ''He's a Sydney Duck. One of the worst of 'em.''

Hume had been very interested, but more restrained. ''So, he was a Duck. But can we be certain that he's the man behind these robberies? Perhaps he's reformed, perhaps he's turned over a new leaf. I've checked with our drivers, and with people who've dealt with Logan. They speak highly of him.''

''I saw the man,'' Raider insisted. ''I looked into his eyes. He's the one we're after.''

''Perhaps,'' Hume replied; ''but we can't put a man in prison because of his eyes, Sydney Duck, or no Sydney Duck. Are you sure that's not why you're really after Logan? Because he was a Duck?''

A good question; one Raider had to think about. His own experiences with Sydney Ducks had been painful, including an old bullet wound, and some knife scars. One didn't forget reminders like that. One didn't forget men like Logan.

The first of the Sydney Ducks had arrived in California back in the early fifties, at the height of the gold rush, attracted by the prospect of appropriating their share of all that new wealth. Most of them had come, as their names implied, from Sydney, in Australia. Only sixty years before the gold rush, the English government had organized southeastern Australia, New South Wales, as a vast prison colony, a way to rid England of her unwanted elements. Many of the prisoners had been sentenced to harsh terms for crimes as petty as stealing a loaf of bread. Other prisoners had been transported to Australia for much more vicious crimes; there were highwaymen, assassins, poisoners, and thugs.

After the prisoners had served their sentences, they were free to leave New South Wales if they could afford it. Most stayed in Australia; they had little choice. A few returned to England. Others fanned out through the world, forming an international criminal element, spawned in a colony of criminals. As a group, Raider had never met a worse collection of cutthroats. For years they had dominated prostitution, gambling, robbery, and extortion in the West. Better law enforcement had forced most to leave for better pickings, but a few had stayed in California. Some turned to honest work, but others, and Raider was certain that Logan was in this category, merely became less blatant in their lawlessness, more clever.

But Hume had a point. How would they prove that Logan was running a gang of robbers?

"A decoy," Raider murmured, mostly to himself. "We'll send in a decoy. Set the bastard up, like he's been settin' us up."

"What?" Hume asked, having barely heard Raider.

Raider looked up. He became more animated. "We'll fix the mistake we made before, when we told too many people 'bout that fake gold shipment. This time, only Logan will be told. And when he acts—"

"If he acts."

"He will," Raider said with great conviction. "I'm sure of it."

However, his certainty was not shared by either the Pinkerton National Detective Agency, or Wells Fargo. Particularly Wells Fargo. Logan's inn was one of the most important stops on their route to Los Angeles. He had, by wining, dining, and flattery, impressed some of the stagecoach company's managers. Or perhaps simply paid them off. Either way, they refused to mount an operation against their friend, Logan.

Yet the idea had lodged itself firmly in Raider's mind. That day when he'd passed by the inn he'd seen the friendly attention Logan paid to the two Wells Fargo drivers. But he'd also looked into Logan's icy eyes during an unguarded moment when Logan had not been playing a role. Raider was willing to bet his life that Logan was the man they were looking for, but to set him up, he'd have to go it alone. If no one else would help, he'd set the trap by himself. Which would indeed be betting his life.

He told Hume nothing, but once again he slipped away from Caliente, alone, in the early morning. This time he was dressed a little more prosperously, but not too much more richly than the last time he'd passed by the New South Wales Inn. Even though their eyes had met for only a few seconds, he was certain that Logan would remember him. Logan had not survived this long by making mistakes. Or by forgetting faces.

Raider took his time on the trip, wanting to save his horse's strength as much as possible. He reached the inn during the late afternoon of the second day. When he dismounted, a hostler came out to take his horse. Real fancy service. The hostler was about to lead the horse away, when Raider stopped him. "Hand me down my saddlebags," he ordered the man. The hostler seemed surprised at the request, but when he was slow in complying, Raider insisted again, showing annoyance at the delay, and perhaps even a little alarm at the prospect of being separated from his saddlebags for even the few minutes it would take to go inside the inn and register for a room.

Sour-faced, the hostler unslung the bags. His expression turned to surprise when he felt their weight. Raider quickly took the bags, then went into the inn. A bored clerk sat slumped behind a counter, but snapped to a semblance of attention when Raider came into the room. It was a fair-sized room, furnished with comfortable chairs, couches, and with brightly-polished brass cuspidors scattered between the potted plants. Raider was impressed. The New South Wales Inn was a much better-looking establishment that one might expect to find in such an otherwise drab area. Even the reception counter was of rich, dark, well-polished wood.

Raider rented one of the more expensive rooms. A dollar and a half a night. During the negotiations he kept asking the clerk if the room was secure. The clerk eyed the obviously heavy saddlebags Raider was lugging, and assured him that it was the most secure room in the house.

It was not until Raider turned away from the desk that he saw Logan, half-hidden in shadow, just the other side of a wide archway that led into what looked like a dining room. Logan was standing, motionless, obviously observing him. Before Raider could say anything, Logan stepped back out of sight behind the archway.

Raider went back out to his horse, accompanied by a porter, who carried in his two rifles and his bedroll. Raider still held tightly to his saddlebags. He followed the porter to the rear of the hotel, where he was shown into a large, well-furnished room. Raider took one look at the room's single, large window, which reached almost to the ground outside, and insisted that this would not do. "The clerk downstairs said that this room was secure. It's not. Anyone could come in through that window."

"Were you expecting anyone in particular, sir?" the porter asked acidly.

"None o' your damned business," Raider snapped back. "Now, either find me a better room, or tell whoever owns this place I want my money back."

Apparently they wanted his money, probably in more ways than one, Raider thought cynically, because they quickly found him a room on the second floor, with a much smaller window, many feet from the ground. He professed satisfaction, then tipped the porter fifty cents, which bought him a smile. It was not until after the porter had left the room and closed the door that Raider finally put down the saddlebags. They made a dull, metallic chinking sound as they hit the bed. He smiled. He'd bought several boxes of extra ammunition before he'd left Caliente, and poured the cartridges loose inside the saddlebags. All that lead made the bags damned heavy. Almost as heavy as if they contained gold.

So far, so good. He'd made certain that everyone noticed the weight of the saddlebags, then he'd reinforced the image of a nervous, gold-laden traveler, by showing how jealous he was of keeping those heavy bags in his constant possession. He hoped he hadn't overdone it.

Well, here he was, and as long as he had a dollar and a half invested in the room, he might as well use it. An oak commode with a marble top stood against one wall. A china pitcher full of water rested on a small shelf next to the commode. Stripping off his shirt, Raider washed off as much trail dirt as he could reach. When he was itching a little less, he put his shirt back on, then picked up the saddlebags and his Winchester and went downstairs.

There were already other guests in the dining room. Raider sat down at a table near a wall, with his back against the wall. His rifle attracted some curiosity, but not much. This was, after all, one hell of a rough area, and when the other diners heard the solid metallic clink as Raider put his saddlebags down onto the floor next to his chair, they understood.

Raider had to admit that the New South Wales Inn served a decent dinner, perhaps a little heavy on meat and potatoes, but he liked meat and potatoes. As he was sopping up the last of the gravy with a thick chunk of fresh bread, the waiter tactfully mentioned that there was a small bar just the other side of the reception desk, where brandy and other strong spirits were served. "Don't mind if I do," Raider said, belching politely.

As he walked into the little bar, he saw Logan leaning nonchalantly against the wall. He thought he saw Logan's eyes flicker slightly as he clanked the saddlebags down onto the bar. "Whiskey," Raider said to the bartender.

"This one'll be on me, stranger," Logan said. "New guests always get the first drink on the house."

Particularly if they're carrying bags of gold, Raider thought, but aloud, he thanked Logan. "Guess you own this place."

"Right you are, mate."

The "mate" came out as "might." Raider was surprised. Considering the bad reputation of the Sydney Ducks, he would have expected Logan to make every effort to lose his Australian accent—if it was indeed possible to do so. However, the man had a pleasing voice, which made the harshness of the accent easier on the ear. Logan smiled, then came to the bar to stand near Raider. "Haven't I seen you somewhere before?" Logan asked.

Raider nodded. "Prob'ly. I passed through this way several weeks ago, headin' down toward Los Angeles."

"But you didn't stay with us."

"Nope. Too early in the day, an' I had a lotta miles t' cover."

Logan changed the subject. Raider let Logan draw him out bit by bit. He was smooth, very smooth; friendly but not imposing, apparently content to listen more than talk, which was always flattering. But more than once, when Logan did not think he was watching, Raider caught a glimpse of what he had seen that one other time, the icy light in those cold gray eyes. Feral eyes. The eyes of a man-eater.

Raider's story was simple: He was a cattleman from the northern part of the state. Having worn out his land, he'd sold his herd, and was now on his way down to the Los Angeles area, to look for new land. When he mentioned selling a herd, Logan's eyes moved involuntarily toward the saddlebags.

"Are you staying with us long, mate?" Logan asked idly.

"Nope. Pushin' on in the mornin'."

Logan stayed another few minutes, then excused himself. Raider watched him go, a tall man, heavily-built, but not fat. A man who walked like a large, dangerous cat.

Raider ordered several more drinks, most of which he poured into a cuspidor when he was certain that no one was watching. Weaving a little, he started to leave the bar, then, as if belatedly aware of their absence, he came running back to snatch his saddlebags off the bar top.

He did not sleep easily that night. He knew that he was in a dangerous place; he could smell it all around him. He wondered why no one else could sense it, why this place was not shunned. Perhaps others did not feel as he felt, simply because they were not targets. Most people who passed through the New South Wales Inn were not supposedly carrying a fortune in gold in their saddlebags.

Before lying down, he pushed a heavy dresser in front of the room's single door. He doubted that any real attempt would be made on him here in the hotel; that would only draw attention to the place. Still, if he could be made to completely vanish during the night, who would notice?

He awoke in the morning still in one piece, having slept a little toward dawn. He washed again, picked up his Winchester and saddlebags, then went downstairs. Although it was only a little after dawn the dining room was doing a thriving business. He ate little, concentrating on the coffee, which was strong and hot, acting like a man who had drunk far too much the night before. Then, calling for the porter, he had his bedroll and Sharps brought downstairs. He had already made arrangements for his horse; it was waiting outside the door, saddled and bridled. He fastened his gear in place, including the saddlebags, then mounted, and rode away. He looked back at the inn once, and thought he saw Logan watching him from an upstairs window.

When he was a mile from the inn, well out of sight, he dismounted and carefully checked his horse gear, item by item, looking for cut girths, burrs under the saddle blanket, weakened reins, whatever might make him less than an effective fighting machine.

He found it tightly wedged between his horse's hoof and the shoe, a small sliver of metal that would have eventually worked its way in deep, laming the animal. He very carefully pried the piece of metal free, then used a smooth rock to hammer the shoe back on, nice and tight.

It made him angry that they had tried to lame such a fine animal, but at the same time he was a little relieved. Now he was sure that he'd been right, that Logan was the man they were after. The question was, where would it happen? Where would they hit him? Remounting, he rode carefully, constantly scanning the terrain on both sides of the trail, far ahead. Certain places he dismissed as completely unsuitable for an ambush, and he rode straight on by. Those places which promised concealment for hidden attackers received considerably more scrutiny.

That was how he pinpointed where the men were hiding. About a quarter mile ahead, the trail narrowed, with a dense growth of trees pressing in from either side. A fine place for bushwhacking. And there! The loud cawing of crows, followed a moment later by the sight of two of the big black birds flapping heavily into the air from a treetop, angrily cursing something that had disturbed them.

From here to the trees, the trail wound and curved. If there was anyone waiting under those trees, they would have already spotted Raider. But a few yards ahead of where he was now, the trail wound out of their sight, screened by thick brush. They would lose sight of him for a while, until the trail broke into the open again, only a hundred yards or so from where the crows had left the trees.

The country was hilly. It was easy for Raider to leave the trail and head up a small gully that would take him behind the trees. He rode carefully but quickly, trying not to make too much noise, but also wanting to close distance before whoever might be waiting ahead began to wonder what had happened to him.

He came out of the gully above and behind the two bushwhackers. They were hunkered down behind a small grassy rise, under thick trees, just thirty yards off the trail, Each man held a rifle. Both rifles were aimed at the trail, at a point which Raider should have reached by now.

Raider slipped off his horse and reached for a rifle. Which one? The Sharps or the Winchester? With the Sharps he could probably kill both men without giving them much chance of hitting him. But dead men don't talk, and he wanted very badly to talk to both of them.

It would have to be the Winchester, a better weapon for close range fighting. Raider pulled the rifle from its saddle scabbard, then started downhill on foot, heading toward the two men. The first couple of hundred yards would be the most dangerous; he would have to cross some fairly open ground. If they discovered him too soon, they would be able to slip back into the trees, and open up on him from behind good cover, while he remained exposed.

Moving carefully, avoiding every dry twig and every pile of leaves, Raider worked his way downhill. Fortunately, the men had all their attention focused on the trail. However, as time passed, and their intended victim failed to materialize out of the brush further down the trail, they began to grow nervous. Raider could see them fidgeting. One leaned close to the other and whispered something into his ear.

When Raider was only about fifty yards away, one of the men stood up. "I don't care what you say, Ted," he growled in a tone clearly audible to Raider. "There's somethin' wrong. Either that gent fell off his nag, or he heard them damn crows and rode off."

Or he's right behind you, Raider thought.

"So what?" Ted replied. "Either way, we wait—maybe another five minutes. If he don't show by then, we light on out. That'd be too damned bad. They said he was carryin' so much gold he could hardly walk."

The other man flopped back down onto the ground. "If'n I catch that bastard in my sights, he ain't gonna do no more walkin' at all."

So, they'd planned on just gunning him down. Raider thought of all the lonely travelers, less forewarned, who must have lost their lives along this trail. A momentary flash of anger distracted him. His foot came down on a twig just as the bored whinny of his horse floated down from far above. Both gunmen twisted around at the same moment, instantly bringing their rifles to bear. Damn, but they were fast!

Raider did not have a chance to fire; both bandits already had their rifles up and were aiming at him. He threw himself to the side, behind a small rise. Below, both bandits fired almost simultaneously. Bullets whizzed by, one of them nicking the crown of Raider's hat.

He hugged the ground. The little rise he was hiding behind was not more than two feet high, barely giving him cover. Nor was it very long, it petered out to ground level another ten yards to his right

He poked his head up. He had time to catch only a glimpse of the bandits before they fired again. He dived back down, hearing the bullets whine by overhead.

During that one brief look, he'd been able to see that the bandits were splitting up, one going to the right, the other to the left. Good thinking. They'd close in on him from the sides, and gun him down the moment they'd flanked his cover.

Time to move, if he could do so without stopping a bullet. Almost immediately another bullet whizzed by, making his hat rock a little. Maybe that was the answer; the crown of his hat stuck up a little above the rise of ground; it helped them pinpoint his position.

Or so they thought. Raider carefully worked the hat off his head, leaving it in place. Then he began to crawl toward his right, pressing his belly hard against the earth. He had only gone a few yards when he heard stealthy footsteps approaching from the right. He hoped it was only one of them.

He could see a little ahead, to a patch of brush. His hand closed around a rock. He rolled the rock along the ground, right into the brush. The moment he heard the rock reach the brush, he rolled to his right, away from the rise that had so far protected him. Then he leaped to his feet.

One of the bandits, the one called Ted, was standing only a few yards away, with his rifle covering the patch of brush the rock had rolled into. He saw Raider immediately, and started to turn.

No time for the Winchester. Raider reached for his Colt, cocking the hammer as the pistol slid from its holster. He fired an instant before the bandit, his bullet slamming into Ted's body just in time to ruin his aim.

It was not a good hit, the bullet had only struck Ted in the shoulder, but it had spun him partway around, and he was slow in turning back toward Raider. Raider shot him through the head. Ted's rifle flew into the air, and he fell on his back, right into the middle of the bush where Raider had thrown the rock. He remained flat on his back, with his legs jerking spasmodically. He was already dead.

A cry came from behind Raider. He turned just in time to see the other gunman running toward him, already raising his rifle to his shoulder. Raider's rifle was still in his left hand. He dropped his pistol and brought the rifle up to firing position. The other man was already firing, but not accurately. He had been too foolish, or perhaps too angry over the death of his partner, to have the presence of mind to stop his forward charge. Firing a rifle while running full speed is not particularly effective.

Forcing himself to hold steady even as bullets were whining around him, Raider aimed and fired. The bandit was about fifty yards away when Raider's first bullet hit him. He staggered, but kept on coming. Another bullet hit him in the leg, and he went down hard, but he did not lose his hold on his rifle.

Now it became a matter of timing. Raider was already running toward the fallen bandit, hoping he could reach him before he recovered enough strength to fire again. But it was not to be. Raider saw the wounded man push his rifle out in front of him, then start to sight down the barrel. Lying prone, with the earth as a steady rest, he should be able to hit Raider easily.

But he was slow. Raider skidded to a stop, raised his rifle, and fired. He saw the bandit's body jerk. His back arched spasmodically. Raider began to run again. This time the bandit made no move to fire, but lay completely still.

He was dead when Raider reached him. That last bullet had entered his body near the neck, and since he'd been lying prone, the bullet had continued down into his body, traveling the long way, exploding his heart before it finally came to rest.

Raider swore in disgust, and kicked a clump of dirt onto the dead bandit. Damn it all! Another potential witness lost. As he'd recognized earlier, dead men can't talk.

CHAPTER ELEVEN

Raider paced up and down the railroad station platform, his mind seething with unvoiced curses. How the hell could they do this? How the hell could they set a Goddamned spy on him?

Lack of progress, they had curtly stated, in reply to his angry telegram. Hell, the lack of progress wasn't his, it was theirs! He'd reported his experience at the New South Wales Inn, how he'd set up Logan, the ensuing robbery attempt, the death of the two bandits. Nothing. They'd done nothing. Even Hume had not been much help. He'd been interested, of course, even fascinated, but cautious. "Sounds like you might be right," he'd told Raider. "Logan may be our man. But without a little more solid evidence— Damn. It's a shame neither of those two bushwhackers lived to talk."

"Yeah. But I cain't bring 'em back t' life, can I?" Raider replied sourly.

"Are you sure they were from Logan? From what you told me about this man, Leonis, over Calabasas way, he could have been gunning for you, too."

"Damn it!" Raider burst out. "I heard the bastards say they'd been told I had a bagful of gold! The only one who could've told 'em that was Logan."

Hume shrugged. "Or anyone in his employ. There's little

doubt that there's something fishy going on at Logan's place. But as for pinning it on Logan himself—''

"What that bastard needs is a hemp necktie."

"If we can get the evidence, that's what he'll be wearing. We're going to play this carefully, warn the men to be cautious about what they say when they pass through Logan's place."

"The word'll get 'round. He'll run," Raider muttered.

"Fine. Then we'll go after him."

And that's where it had been left, until there were two more robberies. The day after the second robbery, the agency had telegraphed a message that they were sending Raider an assistant. A man named Thomas. Jefferson Thomas. More likely it was some agency fink meant to keep an eye on him, so that he could report back whether or not Raider was losing his touch. Well, by God, if this Jefferson Thomas tried to interfere with the way he worked—

Raider was extremely touchy about working with someone else, after Doc. For years he'd had a partner, Doc Weatherby, a little dude from Boston. He and Doc had fought like siblings, but eventually that was what they had become; nearly brothers. Then Doc had to go marry that rich eastern bitch. Since then, Raider had grown used to working alone. He liked the freedom of being his own man, of making his own decisions, all the decisions. And now—well, he'd put this damn spy in his place, let him know that nobody interfered with the way Raider worked a case.

The train was coming now, smearing its plume of dirty black smoke against the colorless Caliente sky. Accompanied by a great shrieking of brakes, it chuffed to a stop at the station platform. Raider leaned back against the station wall, arms crossed, watching the passengers as they began to disembark, on the lookout for any icy-eyed individual with the heart of a snake. What the hell else kind of man would spy on a fellow operative?

After a few minutes he began to wonder if his man might have missed the train. Most of the passengers were already on the platform. They were a motley bunch: an old couple; a man and woman around thirty years old; a greenhorn kid from the East; and, well, one that wasn't too hard to look at, a woman, maybe in her middle to late twenties, dressed to the nines. She was looking around the platform as if someone had failed to meet her. If someone didn't show up for her pretty damn soon, maybe it would be interesting to see if he couldn't give her a little personal traveler's aid.

Raider was so engrossed in admiring the woman that he did not pay much attention to the man, until he spoke, almost in Raider's ear. "Mister Raider—sir?" a male voice said deferentially

Raider's head swiveled away from the woman. The greenhorn Eastern kid was standing just a yard or so away, holding his hat in his hand, a damned silly hat, the kind a writer of dime Westerns might hang on his paper hero's head. The kid was shuffling his feet, and looking at Raider with huge, puppy-dog eyes. Could it be? Was this the help they'd sent him?

Raider grunted some unintelligible assent to the young man's question. The kid kept right on talking. "You look just like they said you'd look, Mr. Raider," he said, his voice hushed, as if he were a nun talking to the pope. "I recognized you right off. I—"

"You're Thomas?" Raider managed to choke out. "Jefferson Thomas?"

"Yessir. But everybody calls me Jeff. I hope you will too, Mr. Raider."

"Cut that mister shit!" Raider snapped. "I'm just Raider. Plain ol' Raider."

The glow in Jeff's eyes indicated that, to him, there was nothing at all plain about Raider. What kind of stories have they been telling about me back there? Raider wondered. He took a closer look at the kid. He was tall, lean, strong enough, but, under a shock of curly blond hair, he wore one of the most innocent faces Raider had ever seen. God! They'd

saddled him with a greenhorn! "Why the fuck are you here?"
Raider said from between clenched teeth.

Not only the words, but the tone of Raider's voice set Jef
back a little. "Why, they—ordered me to come. I—"

"No. I mean, why? For what purpose?"

"Well—they said that I needed a little seasoning. Mis—uh
Raider. That you were the man to do it."

"Great. Fine. Just great," Raider snarled. He was right in
the middle of one of the most difficult cases he could remem
ber, and they were setting him up to be a Goddamn nursemaid.

Well, no point in kicking against the rope. The kid wa:
here, he was stuck with him. "You got any gear?" he aske
Jeff.

"Sure. There's a trunk in the baggage car—"

A trunk. The kid was traveling with a trunk. "I hope yo
got some other clothes in it," he grated. It made his skin itcl
to be seen with anybody dressed the way Jeff was dressed: ;
bizarre approximation of the way most Easterners probably
figured a Western gunman dressed; tight, fancy trousers, ;
checked vest, a silk shirt with a string tie, and boots so shin
and fancy that they hurt Raider's eyes. And that hat. A real
twenty-gallon model, with a brim so wide that he wondered
how the kid managed to get through doors.

He'd draw attention. He'd make the both of them as con
spicuous as hell. But, on the other hand, maybe he'd better
leave the kid's clothes alone. They were a kind of disguise.
Nobody would ever take Jefferson Thomas for a Pinkerton
agent.

They corralled the kid's trunk. It was a medium-sized
trunk, and apparently rather heavy, but he noticed that Jeff
slung it up onto his shoulder with little effort. Well at least
the kid was strong.

He made certain that Jeff checked into the hotel alone, so
that the two of them would not be so easily connected. That
night he and Hume came to Jeff's room for a planning
session. Jeff mostly listened, his awe partitioned between

aider, a Pinkerton legend, and Hume, the ex-sheriff of angtown, who was a legend in his own right.

"What I suggest," Hume said, "is that we put some subtle essure on Logan. Let him know that we're on his trail. Maybe that'll spook him, make him do something that'll help s connect him to the robberies. Of course, there's always the anger that he'll just lie low for a while, give us nothing at l."

Raider scratched his head. "Mebbe not. The Logan I met not the kind of man to defend himself by sittin' still. If he els threatened, he'll do somethin' positive 'bout it."

So the plan was set. The next morning Raider once again t out from Caliente, outfitted for the trail. He left alone; the lan called for Jeff to meet him about five miles from town. eaching the meeting place first, Raider looked around for a uiet spot from which he could observe the trail. He rode nder some trees, and dismounted, then he sat down on a rock to ait. About ten minutes later he heard the muffled clopping f a horse's hooves against the dirt of the trail. Shortly ereafter, a most amazing apparition hove into view. "God-amn," Raider murmured. "Buffalo Bill an' Wild Bill Hickock ll rolled into one."

Jeff was indeed a resplendent sight, decked out in tight Mexican-style trousers with a stripe running up the outside of ae legs; a fringed buckskin jacket; that incredible, wide-rimmed hat; those shiny boots, which sported a set of the iggest spurs Raider had ever seen; and to top it off, a pair of rossed gun belts holding up twin, pearl-handled revolvers.

Raider stepped out onto the trail, scaring the hell out of eff. "R-Raider," he stammered, struggling with his equally tartled horse.

"Who were you expectin'?" Raider replied drily. "Jesse ames?" He did notice, though, that the kid was handling his orse well enough. Sighing, he got back on his own horse, nd together they rode on down the trail, Raider casting ccasional glimpses at the apparition riding beside him.

They reached the Newhall area late that day, not far from

the New South Wales Inn. They left the trail a couple
miles short of the inn, then rode up into the hills. Raider le
the way, searching for a high point he'd seen earlier, fro
below, when he'd stayed at the inn. They found it a litt
before dark. Dismounting, Raider walked cautiously to
small crag, near the top of the high point. Getting down o
his knees, he looked over the edge. "Perfect," he murmured
The New South Wales Inn lay below them, about two hur
dred yards away.

Time to settle in. Raider led them about a quarter of a mil
away from the rise, to a small glade that was far enough fro
the main trail, and with enough ground cover to protect ther
from being easily spotted. Here they set up camp. Raide
gave Jeff no direct orders, but observed him, admitting grudg
ingly that the kid did a fair job of finding himself a nice littl
depression, filling it with pine needles, and ending up with
decent bed. Both men propped their slickers on frames mad
of cut saplings, forming a roof over their bedrolls. Might a
well make the camp comfortable; they could be here for som
time.

Jeff's problems started soon enough. The huge rowels o
his spurs caught on everything he passed. Once, when
rowel caught in a protruding root, he fell flat on his face
Raider managed to hide a snicker, but nodded later when th
kid had the sense to take off his damned spurs and tuck ther
away in his saddlebags.

They ate a cold meal of beans and hardtack. There could b
no fires here; their camp might be spotted. Raider had neve
liked cold camps, although he'd put up with enough of them
He was pleased that Jeff did not complain. Neither of ther
said much. They were both in their bedrolls within an hou
after dark.

And up an hour before first light. Leaving the horse
securely staked out, both men walked to their observatio
point. They were in position as the first lights came on in th
buildings below them. Raider studied the scene through hi
binoculars. The New South Wales Inn awoke very slowly

First, the cooks and their helpers shambled into the kitchen. Soon, their labors were sending the first plumes of woodsmoke into the otherwise clear sky. Then the hostlers took charge of the horses, and while the horses nickered, and nipped at one another, other employees staggered out of their sleeping quarters.

The first traveler came out of the main building shortly afterward, mounted his horse, and rode off. Raider hoped that the man's journey was more peaceful than his own had been, when he'd last left the New South Wales Inn.

He caught his first sight of Logan about eight o'clock. Logan came out of the main door, and stood just outside the doorway, where he surveyed his little empire for ten minutes, standing arrogantly, with his arms crossed over his chest.

Raider passed the binoculars to Jeff. "That's our man," he said. "Memorize his face, the way he walks, everything about him. I want you to be able to recognize him even if he's got a sack over his face and is all dolled up in a hoop skirt."

Jeff nodded, then settled down with the glasses, never looking away from Logan for the rest of the time he stood outside the doorway.

The surveillance continued for three more days. Not much out of the ordinary happened below their vantage point. Travelers came and went. The Wells Fargo stages stopped for water and food once each day, one going in each direction. Raider noticed that the drivers and guards were not chumming up to Logan the way they had before. Hume must have given them the word.

Jeff had a painful adaptation to life as an observer. One of the worst problems came from those tight charro style trousers. They were just not suited to wriggling around in the brush, on stony ground. Nor was that fancy fringed jacket. The fringes, which were way too long, kept getting caught in the brush. By the second day Jeff had dug into the pile of clothes that he'd brought inside his oversized bedroll, and furnished himself with a pair of baggy old jeans, and a denim jacket.

One of Jeff's pistols was temporarily retired. Two large-caliber six-guns, housed in a fancy, heavy, leather rig, with each crossed belt stuffed full of heavy cartridges, was just too much weight to lug through the brush. Jeff ended up with one pistol stuck into his belt, and a pocketful of cartridges.

Of course the hat had to go. It was just too huge; it would have stuck up over the edge of their little crag like a warning beacon. All in all, by the third day, Raider had to admit that the kid was looking almost human.

He did talk, though, endlessly pumping Raider for information and anecdotes about his life as a Pinkerton operative. Raider was both annoyed and a little flattered. He found himself talking back a little more than he'd have liked to.

On the fourth day the time for talking ran out. Watching from above, Jeff and Raider watched five hard-looking men, every one of them well-armed, ride into the yard in front of the inn. Their demeanor and their arms branded them as either bandits or lawmen; there was often little difference.

Through the binoculars, Raider caught a glimpse of Logan, watching the newcomers from an upstairs window. His face disappeared from the window, and a couple of minutes later he appeared in the front door. The strangers had made no move to come in, or even to dismount. They'd said a few words to a hostler; Raider could imagine them having asked for Logan, perhaps even demanded his presence. If Raider was right, Hume had sent these men. They were part of the general plan. Their job was to light a fire under Logan's arrogant ass. They would accomplish this by alluding to a murder that had never taken place, except in Logan's mind.

When Raider had killed the two bandits, the ones he was certain Logan had sent after him, he'd dragged their bodies beneath a high cutbank. Using the barrels of the dead mens' rifles, he'd caved the cutbank down on top of their corpses. He'd led away the bandits' horses, which he'd found hidden in a little copse of trees. When he'd ridden far enough, he'd hidden the horse gear in the brush, then let the horses loose.

here was a settlement about a half mile away; the horses ould smell fodder and head in that direction.

Thus, both bandits and victim would seem to have vanshed right off the face of the earth. Raider hoped that Logan ould think that the bandits had killed him and ridden on, heating Logan out of his share of the loot. So, enter Hume's nen. Right about now they should be asking Logan some ointed questions about the man who'd passed through he New South Wales Inn a while before. A man carrying fortune in gold. A man who had not been heard from nce.

Of course, Logan would claim no knowledge of the man's ate. Raider could see him now, standing relaxed as he talked the men, his face cool and composed. If Hume's men were ollowing the plan, they would make no direct accusations, ut their faces would be tight, suspicious, unconvinced.

Finally, still not having dismounted, the men turned their nounts and departed, rather rudely, Raider thought, leaving Logan standing alone in front of the door to his inn. An inn hat was now apparently suspect.

Raider saw Logan lose his composure for just a moment, icking angrily at a weed that grew near a pump. There must e a lot going through his mind. First off, the unexpected oolness of the Wells Fargo men. Now, the hard eyes of the trangers who'd just visited him, and their even harder quesions. Raider suspected that Logan had grown complacent ver the past few years, overconfident. It had been a long ime since he'd been an object of direct suspicion. Now, aving been goaded a little, how would he react?

Raider got his answer about ten minutes later, when Logan, who had gone inside, abruptly appeared again, dressed and utfitted for the trail. He and Jeff watched Logan order a man o fetch him a horse. Logan fidgeted while the horse was eing saddled and bridled. Raider could see Logan's mouth noving, could imagine him chewing out the hostler, telling im to move faster.

Raider put down the glasses, then turned to face Jeff, who was watching him, questions written all over his open, guileless face. "Looks like our bird's got his wind up," Raider said drily. "Let's see which way he flies."

CHAPTER TWELVE

Raider sent Jeff back to break camp and saddle the horses, while he stayed on the hilltop, watching Logan ride away from the inn. He was glad he'd decided to stay; he'd expected Logan to turn left onto the main trail, which would have taken him toward Los Angeles. Instead, he turned right. Would he head toward Caliente?

Raider loped back toward camp. Jeff met him halfway, riding his horse and leading Raider's. A quick check indicated that Jeff had packed everything the way Raider liked it. Raider nodded. Apparently the kid was a good observer.

Swinging wide of the inn, they struck the main trail about a half mile north. It took Raider just a few minutes to locate the tracks of Logan's horse; only one set of prints had been made this morning. They headed north.

But instead of continuing on toward Caliente and the Central Valley, the tracks turned off to the left about a mile farther along, heading down the river valley Raider had earlier ridden through on his way to the sea. Now why the hell would Logan head west?

There was nothing to do but follow. Which was not always easy. At places the valley opened out enough so that it would be easy for Logan to spot anyone tracking him too closely. Raider and Jeff hung well back, only occasionally catching a faint, fleeting glimpse of their quarry. Raider relied mostly on following the tracks of Logan's horse. Jeff was fascinated by Raider's trailcraft, and kept asking questions. Raider was annoyed at first, but decided that the kid had to learn sometime. "Look there," he said, pointing to a place where the tracks had set well into soft, moist soil. "The right front shoe is bent up a little at one corner. Must bother the horse, 'cause you can see that he favors that leg just a tad. Leaves odd tracks."

Jeff studied the ground carefully. Raider wondered if he was really seeing anything, so he let Jeff do the tracking for a while. To Raider's surprise, the kid only goofed a couple of times. He had phenomenal eyesight.

The day drew on. Even though they had tracks to follow, they could not take anything for granted. There was always the chance that Logan was heading toward someplace or someone here in the river valley. Each possible turning had to be checked out. But Logan continued on, stopping only a couple of times to rest his horse. Once, he actually doubled back on his tracks, as if trying to trap anyone following him. Raider caught sight of Logan in time to grab Jeff's reins, and lead both their horses into dense brush, where they were impossible to spot. Ten minutes later Logan headed west again.

Dark caught Logan about five miles from the sea. Raider had been worried about the day ending. They could easily lose their man in the darkness. Fortunately, Logan made camp for the night. They could see his fire glowing down by the river. They could also, agonizingly, smell his coffee brewing and his bacon cooking, while they ate cold beans out of cans.

"Somethin' strikes me as real interestin'," Raider murmured to Jeff.

Jeff looked quizzical. "What's that?"

"That Logan lit out in the middle of the day. He could've left tomorrow mornin', slept in his own bed t'night, not ended up stuck out here on the trail. Does that tell you anythin'?"

Jeff thought for a moment. "I guess maybe he's in a hurry."

Raider nodded. "Good thinkin'. Yeah. I'd guess that those five gents Hume sent to the inn rattled Logan pretty bad. Let's hope he's rattled enough to start makin' mistakes. Big mistakes."

They took turns sleeping. In the morning both were awake to see Logan break camp and continue on down the trail. He reached the sea at about nine o'clock. Was he going to head south toward the Los Angeles basin?

No. He turned to the right, heading northeast along the shore. The land was bare here. Jeff and Raider had to drop back even farther. Two hours later they passed the little settlement of Carpinteria, in Spanish, The Carpenter's Shop. Another hour, and they were nearing Santa Barbara. Why Santa Barbara, cut off as it was from the railroad and the inland stage lines?

Santa Barbara was a big enough place to give them some problems. Would Logan ride right on out the other side, or was he after something, or someone, in Santa Barbara itself? The only way to find out was to ride into town, something that Raider could not do, not if Logan were there; he'd be recognized instantly.

Which left Jeff. "You ride on in," Raider told him. "Ride right on through town and out the other side. Look for the marks of that bent shoe. If it don't look like Logan rode on out, come on back here. Then we'll try to figger out how to find the son of a bitch."

"Sure," Jeff said. "I'm on my way."

Raider hesitated. He could see the light of excitement in Jeff's eyes, the eagerness to be doing something on his own. "Be careful," he warned him. "Dead heroes don't bring back any information."

Jeff nodded, then turned his horse and rode away toward the town. He looked back, once, to see Raider watching him. He felt a thrill of pride. Damn! If his friends back home could see him now, riding off on a mission for a crack Pinkerton operative. Hell, he was an operative himself! Which was something he had to keep reminding himself of. He could hardly believe all the incredible things that had happened to him over the past few months.

He'd always been interested in detective work, even as a child. He figured he'd bought just about every sleuth novel and how-to-do-it book that was ever published. Then, last year, his big break, the fluke that had gotten him the attention of a local Pinkerton man. He'd discovered a fugitive all by himself, from studying wanted posters in the local post office. He'd personally led the Pinkertons to the man they were after. He'd even helped with the capture.

Instead of accepting the usual money reward, he'd asked—hell, he'd begged them—to give him work, real detective work. Impressed by his zeal, the local men had passed his name on to the Chicago office, and damned if they hadn't hired him in a part-time, local capacity. Well, they hadn't really paid him much, they'd just let him work on some easy cases, helping him out a little with his expenses. And then had come a bank robbery. He'd collared the robber himself. Of course, the bank robber had only been a broken down old bum, but he'd had a gun, and Jeff had walked right up to the robber, kicked the gun out of his hand, and taken him into custody.

That had really gotten their attention. Two months of training had followed at the Chicago head office. He'd been fascinated by the main office's rogues' gallery, but it was field work that he yearned for, real work, chasing down big-time lawbreakers. When Raider had requested the research on Logan, Jeff was the one who'd done the actual work. Later, when he discovered that they were going to send someone out to California to work with Raider—Raider the legend—Jeff had begged and begged until, just to get rid of his nagging, they sent him off.

And now here he was, on his own. Holding himself stiff in the saddle, the thumb of his right hand hooked in his belt so that his hand was close to the butt of the pistol stuffed into his waistband, he rode into Santa Barbara, feeling ten feet tall. He thought regretfully of the fancy clothes tucked away into his bulging bedroll, of the twin, pearl-handled forty-fives in their hand-tooled gun belts. That's what he should be wearing, the costume of a gun-toting lawman.

He had reached the center of town, and was daydreaming about how he would have looked in his fancy gear, when he suddenly caught sight of Logan, walking out of a livery stable. Jeff realized he was staring straight at Logan. He summoned the presence of mind to look away before the other man became aware of his scrutiny.

What to do now? Probably, following orders, he should turn his horse around and ride back to find Raider. Orders were orders, the agency pounded that into the heads of trainees. On the other hand, they also stressed taking the initiative, seizing events.

That's what he'd do. He'd use initiative. Logan was stopping at what looked like a boardinghouse. Jeff guided his horse toward a side street, where he dismounted. Holding his horse's reins, he carefully watched the house, memorizing its location. Maybe Logan was going to stay there, although he had not been carrying his bedroll or saddlebags.

Jeff was still wondering what was happening when Logan came out of the front door of the house, looked up and down the street, then set off along the boardwalk, walking briskly. His route would take him right by Jeff. Jeff began to sweat, wondering if he should pull himself farther away from the street corner. No. That would look suspicious.

Logan solved the problem by turning into the open doorway of a saloon, just a few yards from where Jeff was standing. Jeff hesitated only a moment, then led his horse over to the saloon's hitching rail, tied the reins, and walked on into the saloon.

The light was dim inside. It took Jeff a moment to locate his man. Logan was looking around him uncertainly, as if he too were confused by the poor lighting. Then his eyes fell on a man seated at a table halfway back in the room, near the bar. Logan walked toward the man, calling out, "Jamison. I gotta talk to you."

The man at the table was a big man, bigger than Logan. He even looked big sitting down. He was quite handsome, with wavy brown hair, a thick moustache, and light-colored eyes, maybe blue, although it was hard to tell in the dim light. He was fairly well-dressed, in the manner of a successful stockman who no longer needed to personally ride the range. He was wearing expensive-looking but not fancy trousers, and what appeared to be a silk shirt, with a mohair vest over it. He wore no tie, but managed to look like a man of substance anyhow. The hat that lay on the table in front of him looked expensive.

Logan had called the man Jamison. Now Jamison looked up at Logan in obvious annoyance. "What the hell are you doing here?" he said testily.

"We got trouble," Logan replied, pulling out a chair, and sitting down across from Jamison.

"Yeah?" Jamison said in a challenging manner. "Maybe you do. I don't."

"I wouldn't be so bleedin' sure, mate. Some men came by me place yesterday. They looked like lawmen, an' they were askin' a lot of hard questions. I think they know about us."

Jamison looked around the bar. "Shut the fuck up," he hissed to Logan. "You're talkin' too damned loud."

Logan shrugged, then leaned closer to Jamison. He began to speak again, but in too low a voice for Jeff to hear. So Jeff walked further into the room, picking a place at the bar only a few feet from Jamison's table. The bartender dutifully sidled over toward Jeff. "What'll it be, kid?" he asked.

Jeff flushed at the word, kid. Damn it, he was a grown man! It wasn't his fault if his face had lagged a little behind his body. "Beer," he grunted.

The beer appeared in front of him with commendable speed. Foam slopped over the edge of the glass. Jeff looked at the beer dubiously. During his training, they'd told him that a good operative drank only when absolutely necessary, and then, sparingly. However, things seemed different out here in the field. Raider, for example; he seemed never to have heard of the agency's strictures against alcohol. Or any other strictures. Sighing, Jeff took a sip of his beer. It tasted good.

If Jeff's boyish, innocent, open face was a source of shame to him, it was also an invaluable investigative asset. Particularly at the moment. Looking up from his table, Jamison saw only a harmless kid standing at the bar, one who could not possibly have any interest in what Logan was trying to tell him, so he let Logan spout on. "It's about a man who came through with a load of gold, stuffed into saddlebags," Logan was saying to Jamison, with Jeff able to make out most of the words. "I set a couple of your boys onto him—Ted and Luke. They never came back, and neither did he. I figured they hit him, then took off with the gold, the bastards."

"Yeah," Jamison said. "I haven't seen either one of them for quite a while. They just disappeared into thin air."

Looking over the rim of his beer glass, Jeff was able to study Jamison in the big mirror behind the bar. God, but he was a cold-looking specimen. Eyes like ice. Logan had cold eyes, too, but mean cold. Jamison's eyes seemed to have no emotion in them at all.

"Maybe the three of them killed each other," Jamison was saying. "Have you checked?"

"Yeah. Sent Birk and two others out to poke around on the trail. They didn't find a damned thing. Then these five gents showed up yesterday, askin' questions about this man, said he was missing. They made it plain as the nose on your face that they thought something might be fishy with the inn, with me. On top of that, the Wells Fargo people have been giving me the cold shoulder lately. They suspect. I know they suspect."

"So," Jamison drawled. "You got on a horse and headed straight here. Maybe you led them straight here, too."

Logan flushed. "I'm no greenhorn, Jamison. I checked my back trail. No one followed me."

Jamison's eyes swept over the room. They passed right by

Jeff. The invisible man. "Maybe," Jamison finally said. "Maybe not. I hope we don't have to find out the hard way."

"You think I should go back to the inn?"

Jamison thought for a while. "Well, if you disappear, they'll think you've lit out, that maybe you were guilty after all. On the other hand, if they decide to grab you, it might go wrong for all of us. Maybe you'd better stay around here for a while—out at the ranch. Keep out of sight until we decide what the hell's going on."

He leaned closer. "Besides. There's a big score coming up. I could use your special talents. It could pay off big."

Logan grunted, seemed relieved. "Sounds okay to me. The inn can run itself. I left word that I'd be in Los Angeles for a couple of weeks. Nobody's gonna wonder where I am."

Chairs scraped as the two men got up. Jeff carefully studied the foam on his beer. Not trusting to the mirror, afraid that his eyes might meet either Jamison's or Logan's, he left it up to his hearing as they walked behind him, heading toward the barroom door. He forced himself not to turn around even after he'd heard the swinging doors thud shut. They might be watching.

Five minutes later, Jeff was on his horse again, racing toward where he'd left Raider, loaded down with one hell of a lot of news.

CHAPTER THIRTEEN

"So," Raider mused. "Logan's s'posed to be goin' out to some ranch. He won't be in town."

"That's what I heard. I didn't actually see him go."

Raider and Jeff were sitting on the ground in the center of a little clearing about a mile outside Santa Barbara. Raider had felt an initial flash of annoyance when Jeff had told him he'd disregarded his orders and put himself in jeopardy, but the annoyance was quickly replaced by thoughtfulness. "This man, Jamison," he said. "Sounds kinda like Logan was reportin' t' him. Sounds like Jamison is Logan's boss."

"Well," Jeff hedged, "I wouldn't put it quite like that. Logan was a little rattled, but he doesn't seem like the kind of man who'd crawl for anyone."

"No. But still—I think this man, Jamison, is the key. Now all we gotta do is stick him in a lock an' turn him."

Jeff smiled at Raider's imagery. Then he remembered the emotionless cold of Jamison's eyes. "That key has sharp edges," he muttered.

Raider nodded. "It's up to us t' find out just how sharp."

Jeff went into town again, alone. After prowling around for a couple of hours, he saw Jamison in the saloon again, but no sign at all of Logan. Just before dark he rode back to the little clearing. "I think Logan's gone, all right," he reported.

Jeff and Raider rode into town separately, Jeff about a half hour later than Raider. Jeff bedded down in a cheap rooming house. Raider took a room in one of the better hotels. Jeff had told him that Jamison looked prosperous. The best way to get close to a man was to live like him.

The next morning Raider entered one of the town's better clothing stores and changed his attire, buying a dark suit and two silk shirts with string ties. He decided not to buy a vest; the weather was quite warm. He bought a hat, then spent half an hour slapping it against various objects until some of the newness had worn off. Suitably attired, he spent the next few hours wandering around the town.

It was a pleasant town. Until the gold rush, Santa Barbara had been another sleepy little Spanish pueblo, having grown up around the original Franciscan mission. Later, its location next to the sea, with fertile land all around, had attracted many Yankee settlers. Santa Barbara lay smack in the middle of the coast route that ran from Los Angeles up to San Luis Obispo and points north, so there was considerable trade. All in all, Santa Barbara had most of the requirements necessary for real prosperity.

Raider wondered, then, why there were so many hard-looking men on the streets. Obvious bums and gunmen. Perhaps the southern California disease had spread all the way up here. There were prosperous-looking citizens on the sidewalks, too, but Raider noticed that they stepped warily around the hard cases.

Late in the afternoon, Raider entered the saloon where Jeff had seen Jamison. There was, of course, a card game in progress. After watching for a while, and assessing the participants' skills, Raider decided to sit in. He soon learned that he was playing with the mayor, a prosecutor, a judge, and several prominent businessmen. They played damned well; Raider had to struggle to hold onto his money.

About an hour after Raider had joined the game, a tall, rather handsome man entered the saloon. Raider had first noticed the man out of the corner of his eye, but when the public prosecutor waved a hand, and called out, "Hey, Jamison. Come on over and give us a crack at your bankroll," Raider turned and looked up at the man.

Jeff had been right. Jamison had eyes that went way beyond cold. They were merciless eyes that belied the big smile Jamison was flashing. Jamison came over and sat down at the table, nodding at the players one by one, calling them by name. He stopped when he reached Raider. "Don't think I've had the pleasure," Jamison said amiably, but his eyes were sharp, probing, curious.

"Henderson," Raider replied. "John Henderson."

Jamison nodded amiably. "Meriwether Jamison. But most people are kind enough to forget the Meriwether and just call me Jamison."

Jamison was dealt in, and the playing continued. Slowly, smoothly, Jamison elicited the information that Raider was from Arkansas, that he had made a little money in the hardware business, and was now more or less retired. Raider made sure that the amount of his spurious wealth was kept low; if Jamison was the man behind the robberies, he didn't want to become a target for his gang. Not yet. Not until he'd learned enough about the man to bring him down for good.

Over the next few days, Raider played cards with Jamison several times. When he was not playing cards, he poked and pried, quite carefully, finding out all he could about Jamison. Jeff did the same at his own level. After they'd been in town a week, Raider and Jeff met in Raider's hotel room to compare notes. "The man's a killer," Jeff reported. "Everybody knows it. Nobody does anything about it."

Raider nodded. "So I been hearin'."

One night, a little itchy after a long card game, Raider had visited the local brothel. After he'd casually mentioned Jamison's name, a very bitter young whore described to him how Jamison had gunned down her father on the street, in broad daylight, a couple of years earlier. "Just shot him down like a dog," she whispered, her face tight with hatred. "That pig claimed Paw went for him, but that's a lie. Paw never did have much guts. He sure as hell wouldn't draw on a man with Jamison's reputation.''

"No witnesses?" Raider had asked.

The girl chuckled bitterly. Raider noticed how her agitation made her breasts quiver. She had fine breasts. "Oh, there were witnesses," she said. "Some of 'em said as how Jamison just started callin' Paw names. Then he pulled out his pistol and shot Paw through the head. Paw fell with his hands empty. I'm not even sure he had a gun on him. Probably hocked it for booze.''

"Sounds like plain murder to me. Was there a trial?"

"A trial? Hell no, mister. Not with the judge and the prosecutor and the mayor all in Jamison's pocket. The whole damned bunch of 'em are poker-playin' cronies. The witnesses got leaned on. Most of 'em shut up real fast. One who didn't had his house burned down. Then he shut up like a clam, claimed he didn't see a damned thing.''

The girl looked at Raider suspiciously. "How come you're askin' me all these questions?"

Raider shrugged. "Oh, I've played a few card games with Jamison. There was something about him that made me kind of wonder.''

The girl snorted. "That's healthy thinkin', mister. You just keep on wonderin'. There's one real nasty human bein' inside that bastard. If he decides he doesn't like you, blam! Right through the head.''

"And nobody'll do a thing about it."

The girl shook her head. "Nobody. Nobody can touch Meriwether Jamison. Not as long as he has those crooked politicians in his pocket.''

She shook her whole body. She was naked, lying on a bed next to Raider. The shaking did interesting things to her more fleshy parts. It was a hard shake, as if she were trying to throw off something unpleasant. A moment later her look of bitterness was replaced by a professional smile. "Enough talkin', mister," she murmured, artfully gnawing on her lower lip. "Let's you an' me get down to business.''

Raider took away pleasant memories of that solid young body, but less pleasant memories of the hardness of the girl's mind. The entire experience had filled him with nostalgia for Clarissa and Melinda, way over there in Caliente. But he'd learned a lot. The girl's story was not an unusual one in this part of the country. Santa Barbara, like Los Angeles, seemed to be run by a coalition of gamblers and politicians, who were often the same individuals. The mob of Southern sympathizers who had fled west after the war, plus an influx of riffraff from northern Mexico, had the town by the tail. Men like Jamison, if they had the support of the local power structure, could do pretty much as they pleased.

Jeff had brought even more interesting news to the meeting. "Jamison has an interest in a hotel up near Santa Maria," he reported. "A drunk who used to work for Jamison—until Jamison got mad at the poor bastard one day, pistol-whipped him half to death, then fired him—said people ride in from that direction quite often, then settle down with Jamison for long talks."

Raider slapped his thigh. "Damn! I knew it! That's the connection! I always said there has t' be a link b'tween the southern robberies and the ones up 'round San Luis Obispo. Jamison has information comin' in from both directions, from Logan on the one hand, and from that place up around Santa Maria on the other."

Jeff shrugged. "Sounds like it. But, like Mr. Hume said, how can you prove it? And even if you could, with all the protection Jamison has around here, how could you make it stick? The prosecutor probably wouldn't prosecute, and even if he did, the judge would either let Jamison go, or give him a week or two in the lockup. They're his buddies!"

Raider smiled. "Oh, if we get enough proof, these two-bit local shysters won't be able to do nothin' for Jamison. The agency will bring in big guns from outside, powerful men, who'll nail that son of a bitch's hide t' the barn wall. But first, I've gotta get back t' Hume, get the ball rollin'."

"Fine. And while you're gone, I'll stay here and keep an eye on Jamison."

Raider shook his head. "Too dangerous. You wouldn't fit in."

Jeff smiled. "Sure I would. I heard that they're gonna fire the swamper over at the saloon; he's a worthless drunk. I'll go ask for the job tomorrow morning."

Raider was about to say no, then he realized that, where the kid was concerned, he was beginning to sound like a worried father. Very unprofessional. After all, the kid was a Pinkerton operative, and if the head office trusted him, maybe it was time he started doing the same. Jeff had, after all, not yet made any serious mistakes. Of course, the first one would probably kill him, and— No. Time to stop that kind of thinking. "Okay," Raider said. "That's a good idea. But, if anything interestin' happens, send a wire to me in Caliente."

Raider left before dawn. A couple of hours later, when the saloon had opened its doors for the day's early drinkers, Jeff showed up wearing his baggy jeans, a rumpled old shirt, and a hat that looked like it had been stomped into the dirt, which it had. Despite the state of his clothing, or maybe partly because of it—after all, a saloon swamper was not expected to dress like a duke—Jeff got the job; fifty cents a day plus one meal and a beer. It was actually his face that clinched it for him. The naive honesty shining from Jeff's boyish features gave the saloon's owner hope that this one would maybe, just maybe, steal a little less from him than his other employees.

By now Jeff had discovered his near-invisibility. By the time four days had passed, he was, as far as the saloon's patrons were concerned, just part of the furniture. It rankled a bit; he'd rather be noticed, respected, feared, like Raider. Maybe some day he would, when his face aged a little, when he had some investigative triumphs under his belt.

He was grateful for his invisibility on the fifth day, when Logan stomped his way in through the swinging doors. Jamison was seated at his usual table, for once not playing cards, but drinking alone. Jeff had noticed that Jamison drank one hell of a lot, steadily, all day long. He never looked obviously drunk, but Jeff noticed little things about him, subtle indicators, such as a slight slurring of speech, slowed movements, and those eyes. Maybe the lack of anything human in those eyes meant that Jamison had been made profoundly strange inside by the constant alcoholic intake. Maybe he was a little crazy.

Logan went over to Jamison's table, pulled out a chair, and sat down. "One o' the boys came by the ranch," Logan said, his Aussie accent grating on Jeff's ears. "He said you might have somethin' interestin' cookin'."

"Yeah," Jamison replied. "A real fat haul. But we'll have to move on it fast."

"What do you mean?"

Jamison leaned forward, as if he were going to say something important, but then he noticed Jeff, who was mopping tobacco juice off the floor only a few feet away. For just a moment those flat, dead eyes cleared, then locked onto Jeff. Uh-oh, Jeff thought, feeling himself shrink up inside. Maybe he suspects how hard I've been listening.

But the eyes passed over Jeff, and grew empty again. "Let's go to my room," Jamison said to Logan. "We'll talk there."

Still mopping, Jeff watched the two men head for the swinging doors. Damn. Something big was up, and they'd walked away from him. Still, he knew where Jamison lived; in that fancy boardinghouse Logan had visited the day Jeff followed him into town. And Jamison's room was on the ground floor, near the back, with a window facing out onto a side street.

It was now or never. Pretending that he was on his way to the outhouse behind the saloon, Jeff slipped out the back door, then cut to his right down the alley. The feeling inside his guts, a terrible churning, made him want to spend a little time in the outhouse. But he didn't have any time, and sure, he might be scared, anyone in his right mind would be scared, except maybe Raider, if he was planning to eavesdrop on men like Logan and Jamison, but it was his duty. He was a Pinkerton operative. He only wished he had his pistol, but both he and Raider had decided that it would be out of character for a saloon swamper to pack a pistol.

It was after ten o'clock; the streets were darker than sin. Careful not to step on anything that would make noise, Jeff slipped into the little side street that ran next to Jamison's rooming house. There. A light was going on inside Jamison's room. He watched a flare of bright yellow from behind the curtains as a lamp was turned up too high, then someone trimmed the wick, and the glow faded to a mellow gold.

There were thick bushes next to Jamison's window. Moving slowly, the way he'd seen Raider move, like an Indian, Jeff worked his way right beneath the window. Luck was with him. It was a warm night, and the window was partially open.

"What's so secret?" Logan's voice boomed out, right above him. The voice was so close, so immediate, that Jeff had to inhibit an impulse to jump up and run.

"Keep your voice down," Jamison said, his tone annoyed. "There could be somebody outside."

"Better look, then."

Jeff froze as he heard the window above him slide open another few inches. A moment later Jamison stuck his head outside, into the night, but to Jeff's relief Jamison looked outward, rather than down. "Nothing at all," he said, then pulled his head back inside. The curtains swung shut behind him.

He did not close the window. "Two rich Basque sheepmen just sold out their land and flocks up around Paso Robles," Jeff heard Jamison say. "They're gonna try their luck in the Los Angeles area. They're not the kinda men who trust banks. They're bringing their entire stash with them. And they're riding alone. We'll hit them hard, we'll make sure they don't live to talk, then we'll split up their stake."

"Yeah, fine," Logan replied. "I suppose you got word about all this from your Santa Maria connection."

"Well, there sure isn't much coming from your direction," Jamison growled.

Logan's voice was sharp, annoyed, when he replied. "Too much heat from there now, mate. I told you we was overworkin' the area, that some of it would come back at us some day. And now it has."

"Calm down," Jamison said, his voice slightly conciliatory. "I didn't mean anything personal by it. Just the facts. And now we have a chance to make a little profit."

"So?" Logan asked. "Why call me in? This is part of your northern operation."

"I need you. We're shorthanded. What with those men we lost when Wells Fargo set up that phony gold shipment and ambush, and now, with Ted and Luke disappearing along with that gent you set up, we're in trouble."

Jeff heard a sharp intake of breath from inside the room. When Logan replied, he sounded enraged. "You mean you want me to ride out with the boys?" he burst out. "Do a holdup?"

Jamison's tone of voice, when he answered, was almost wry. "Not just you, old son. Me too. We're that shorthanded."

"Damn. It's been years since I've gone out on a job," Logan muttered. But, now that Jamison had said he'd be going too, he sounded somewhat mollified.

"I understand that those two Basques'll be carrying over a hundred thousand dollars," Jamison said. "And there won't be many of us to split it up. Your share'll be the same as mine."

There was a moment's silence. "Maybe it's worth the risk," Logan said. "Hell, if things stay hot, I could just take my share, say good-bye to the New South Wales Inn, and look for better pickin's someplace else."

"In the old days, you never worried much about risk," Jamison chided.

"I was young and stupid then. Maybe I'm stupid now, but I say, let's do it. Let's relieve those two frogs o' their pokes."

"Fine. I knew I could count on you. Now, go on back to the ranch and get your trail gear together. We'll ride out tomorrow night, when nobody's watching."

There was a scraping of furniture from inside, as if Logan and Jamison were getting up from their chairs. Jeff slipped away from the window, worming his way through the bushes until he was out in the open, then he started walking fast, back toward the saloon. He walked in the back door, tugging at his belt, as if he had indeed just left the outhouse. But the subterfuge was not necessary. He was already back at his mopping when Jamison came in, alone, through the swinging doors.

Jamison sat for another hour, drinking steadily, with the usual lack of obvious effect. Jeff waited and watched, wondering if any more men would come in to talk with him. None did. A little before midnight, Jamison left. Slipping outside, Jeff watched until he was certain that Jamison had returned to his rooming house. Only when he saw the light go out inside the room, when he figured Jamison had gone to bed, did Jeff move away into the street. He'd have to hustle. Time was short, and he had a lot to do if he was to save the lives of two Basque gentlemen who did not trust banks.

CHAPTER FOURTEEN

Jeff immediately headed for the telegraph office. The telegrapher was half asleep next to his key, but jerked awake when Jeff entered. Jeff quickly wrote out a message: "Our friend throwing surprise party tomorrow night. Hope you can make it in time. Bring H and friends."

"Party?" the operator muttered, reading the message. Then he saw the destination. "Caliente? Way over there? Hell, they'll never make it to Santa Barbara in time for no party."

"You don't know my partner," Jeff replied, hoping he wasn't kidding himself. "He'd hate to miss the fun."

With the telegram sent, Jeff went back to his room, but he could not sleep. There probably wasn't much he could do by himself until Raider and Hume got here, he figured. But was he leaving out something important?

He was still thinking when he fell asleep. Various dreams drifted through his head, until eventually he had a particularly vivid one: of horses, shrouded in white. Of horses falling. And then he realized that the white mist that covered the horses was sweat, the horses were all lathered up, they'd been run to death. One by one they fell, and men fell with them.

Jeff sat bolt upright in his bed. Horses! Of course, the horses. Even if Raider and Hume made it here in time, their horses would be played out, Jamison would have the edge.

119

He could not let that happen. It was up to him to make sure there were fresh mounts waiting.

And what about Jamison? He had told Logan that they would leave tomorrow night. Correction. That was tonight now. But leave from where?

Having slept in his clothes, Jeff was downstairs within a few minutes of having awakened. There was bright sunlight outside. Damn, it must be ten or eleven in the morning; he'd slept too long. The saloon—should he go there? They'd want him to work, and he had no time for work today. Unless working would put him close to Jamison and Logan. His head spun. There were just too many things to think about!

He peeked into the saloon over the top of the swinging doors. Jamison was not there. Probably still asleep in his rooming house. Should he watch the house?

No. The horses first. He went to the livery stable. The stable owner looked at his ragged clothes and laughed. "A dozen horses? For you? I'd have to see some cash first, sonny."

Jeff automatically dug into his pockets, but he knew already that he had only a few dollars. He hesitated. Perhaps he should tell the man the truth, that he was a Pinkerton operative, and that the horses were for a Pinkerton posse riding in tonight. The trouble was, the damned grinning asshole probably wouldn't believe him, and even if he did, it might not be a good idea to say anything; the stable owner might be in cahoots with Jamison. If he was, he'd blow the whistle, and then the whole plan would collapse, and he'd probably end up dead, full of bullet holes.

"Later, maybe," Jeff said to the livery man, then he turned and left the stables. Once out on the street, he realized that he was hungry. No point in letting himself get run down, just when he needed all his strength. He went to a cheap little restaurant and ate some fatback and biscuits. The food tasted good, and gave him energy. He wondered how Raider could eat that damned Mexican food. It took the roof right off his mouth, but Raider spooned it down like it was ice cream. He sure did sweat a lot, though, when he ate it.

Trivia. He was getting lost in trivia. And now it was noon, and he hadn't accomplished a thing.

The restaurant had one small, dirty window that faced the street. Through it, Jeff saw Jamison walking along the sidewalk. Would he come into the restaurant? No, he passed on by. He'd probably already eaten at his boardinghouse.

Predictably, Jamison went into the saloon. Jeff mopped up the last of his gravy. Should he head for the saloon? No. The horses were still first priority. But how to get hold of them? Steal? Hell, he'd get himself lynched.

Sheriff. The word popped right into his mind. Both he and Raider had taken a little time to study the local sheriff. While he might not be quite the kind of lawman that Hume was, he seemed relatively honest. Or maybe he didn't have much chance to be dishonest; he was not part of the tight little power group to which Jamison and the mayor, the judges, and the prosecutor belonged. Jeff knew that the sheriff hated Jamison, hated all of them.

Finding the sheriff was not an easy proposition. Finally, Jeff was able to pry the information from a sleepy deputy, with the aid of a silver dollar, that the sheriff was taking his afternoon exercise over at the whorehouse. Jeff immediately hied himself in that direction, and ran into more trouble. To most of the locals, he was now the saloon's swamper, and this was a middling to good class whorehouse. "Clean up, sonny, and come back later," the bouncer said, sniggering. "Maybe in five years or so."

"I gotta see the sheriff," Jeff insisted, trying to push past.

The bouncer's expression turned nasty. "Now look here, kid, if you're wantin' a bruisin'—"

He was a big man, and he reached out a meaty hand to haul Jeff back, but his sneer turned into a howl, as Jeff, using what he'd learned in that book about Japanese wrestling, threw the man over his shoulder.

The bouncer hit the floor hard. Jeff was halfway down the

front hall before the old frame building had stopped reverberating from the crash. "Sheriff Jones?" he bawled, walking
fast, knowing the bouncer would be after him very soon,
feeling maybe just a little bit mad.

The hallway was lined with doors. The sheriff came out
through one of them, hitching his suspenders up over his
shoulders. He was barefooted, but Jeff noticed that he had a
forty-five stuck into his waistband. "What the hell you yowlin'
about, kid?" the sheriff snarled. "Don't you know when to
leave a man in peace?" He did not look at all friendly.

"I gotta talk to you, sheriff," Jeff said as quickly as he
could. He could hear the bouncer stumbling down the hall
behind him, cursing sulfurously.

"Go home, kid."

The sheriff started to turn away. Jeff could see the lower
part of a naked leg through the partially open door. Apparently Sheriff Jones still had work to do.

Jeff leaned closer to the retreating man. "It's Pinkerton
business," he hissed.

The sheriff stopped, turned in his tracks, and took a long,
appraising look at Jeff. "You wouldn't be playin' no tricks
on me, would you, son? Cause if you—"

"No!" Jeff hissed frantically. "I'm here in Santa Barbara
undercover, working with a man named Raider. We've
discovered— "

Even as he spoke, he knew it was too late. He could hear
the bouncer panting behind him. It would be only a moment
before he was out in the street on his ear, probably with a
busted face.

But the sheriff suddenly held up his hand. "Hold on,
Jake," he said over Jeff's shoulder to the bouncer. "Give me
a few minutes with the kid."

Jeff turned, to look into Jake's rage-reddened eyes. One
big fist was already drawn back, but the sheriff's words had
frozen Jake in place. "Well," he said. "Yeah. Just so he
don't cause no more trouble."

Jake turned and started to walk away, rubbing one lantern

jaw. Then he stopped and turned back toward Jeff. "Say, kid, how'd you do that?" he asked. "I mean, toss me across the room like I didn't weigh nothin' at all?"

"I—I'll tell you later," Jeff replied. Already, the sheriff was motioning him into the room he'd just come out of. Jeff stepped quickly inside, to be faced with an amply built, naked lady, sprawled out on a rumpled bed. Very amply built. His eyes popped a little as he took a quick, involuntary inventory of her assets. Instead of trying to cover herself, the woman grinned, every inch the professional, showing her wares to a prospective client. It was Jeff who reddened and turned away.

"Sophie," Sheriff Jones said to the woman. "Could you step outside for just a moment?"

Sophie pouted. "Well, Stuart, we hardly got started, but, if you insist—"

Jeff thought he was going to pop a blood vessel as the woman stood up, still naked, then casually wrapped a robe around her body, doing just about everything possible to make it a provocative act. Breasts jiggled, hips swayed, eyes batted. Jeff held his breath as all that femaleness swayed out the door, barely covered by a short, almost transparent robe.

The sheriff looked fondly after her. "She's sure somethin', ain't she," he breathed reverently. Then he remembered who had interrupted his afternoon romp. "You say you're workin' with this man, Raider," he said, turning back toward Jeff. "Describe him to me." Both his voice and his face were very severe.

Jeff ran through a quick inventory of Raider's more noticeable features. Jones nodded. "Sounds like him, all right. Never met him myself, but I've met those who have. You say he's workin' with *you*?"

Jeff flushed. Knowing he was going to have to do some fast convincing, he told the sheriff the whole story, or most of it, as quickly as he could. Sheriff Jones's eyes grew wider and wider. "Jamison?" he finally burst out. "That bastard, Jamison, *he's* in this?"

"Yep."

The sheriff began to rub his hands together. "Oh boy," he muttered. "I got him now. I'll see that son of a bitch swing if it's the last thing I do. I—"

He shot a quick glance at Jeff. "Is there a reward?" he asked.

Jeff nodded. The thought of a reward was probably why the sheriff had originally agreed to talk to him, gambling on even the off chance that he was a genuine Pinkerton. The Pinkertons paid big rewards. All across the nation, hundreds of sheriffs lusted after those rewards. Jeff adopted an official tone. "Both the Pinkerton National Detective Agency, and Wells Fargo too, are paying large amounts of money."

Greed blossomed in the sheriff's eyes. Jeff began to feel real confidence for the first time. "Well, hell, how do we collect these here rewards?" Jones asked, looking a little worried. "I don't know if I could count on raisin' a posse around these parts that would be willin' to take on Jamison."

"There's one already on the way."

Jeff told Jones about the telegram he'd sent, about the need for fresh mounts. The sheriff, after a little cogitation, told Jeff he could probably round up a dozen good animals, but it would take three or four hours. "Now, about the reward," Jones continued. "How do we split it?"

Jeff thought Jones was going to bust a gut when he told him that Pinkerton operatives were not permitted to accept rewards, that all the money would be his. With such a happy prospect ahead of him, Sheriff Jones became a dynamo of activity. "I'll start on the horses," he said while he pulled on his boots. "You go over to the saloon and keep an eye on Jamison."

Sheriff Jones was halfway to the front door before Jeff even realized that he was ready to leave. Jeff figured that it would not be a good idea to be seen in the sheriff's company, so he left at a more leisurely pace, noticing, as he neared the front door, that he got an admiring grin from Jake, but a most offensive scowl from Sophie, who's client he had stolen away.

Jeff nodded to both, then went out into the street, glad he was not wearing Sophie's knife in his back. Once out in the sunlight, he hesitated a moment, then headed toward the saloon. Damn if he wouldn't stick to Jamison like a burr!

But when he entered the saloon, Jamison was nowhere to be seen. Had he gone out back to the outhouse? Jeff put on his stained, ragged swamper's apron, and began sweeping cigar butts toward a large, tobacco-stained spittoon. A half hour later he'd swept the floor as clean as it would ever get, and Jamison still was nowhere in sight. Finally, he got up the nerve to ask the bartender where Jamison had gone. "Oh, him?" the bartender replied. "He left about forty-five minutes ago. He said he was gonna be out of town for a while."

The bartender's forehead wrinkled in thought. "Why the hell do you wanna know, kid? Are you—? Hey! Hey, where the hell are you runnin' off to? You ain't swept behind the bar yet!"

CHAPTER FIFTEEN

Jeff and the sheriff had been riding along the shore for several miles, with the sea on their right. Jeff was nervous; it was damn late in the day. The sheriff, considering it more important to do everything quietly rather than rushing blindly, had taken most of the afternoon to gather the horses, but as soon as they had enough of them, Jeff demanded that they head south immediately, to intercept Raider and Hume and their posse. He knew they were coming; he'd checked at the telegraph office. There had been a terse message, "Wouldn't miss your party for anything. R."

As nervous as he was, Jeff still had time to study his surroundings. Raider had told him how important it was to always know what kind of land lay around you, in case it was suddenly necessary to use the terrain to your advantage.

It was damn pretty here. He could see, far offshore, the rugged outlines of several islands. Looking back over his shoulder, he was dazzled by the bright track the lowering sun made upon the water. An unfortunate reminder, that lowering sun, a reminder of just how quickly time was trickling away. A gang of cold-blooded killers would be riding out soon, to ambush two unsuspecting travelers. They had to be stopped.

The steep mountains that bordered the narrow strip of shore was another reminder of how many extra miles Raider and the posse would have to ride to get around them. The terrain directly between Caliente and Santa Barbara was all but impassable.

Jeff had been slumping a little in the saddle, but he suddenly sat up straighter. Had he seen something further down the road, just at the base of that cliff? He squinted. Yes! A small cloud of dust. Tiny dark shapes were beginning to show through the dust. "I think that's them!" he called out to the sheriff.

Sheriff Jones squinted his eyes in imitation of Jeff, but with less success. "Cain't see a damn thing down that way," he muttered.

"It's them. I'm sure of it now," Jeff insisted triumphantly. "I know the way Raider sits a horse. That's him, all right."

The sheriff could still see nothing where Jeff was pointing except perhaps a slight discoloring of the air, which might be dust. "This kid's got eyes like a hawk," he muttered.

Ten minutes later, the newcomers were in plain sight: Raider, Hume, and ten hard-bitten posse men. As Jeff had anticipated, their mounts were about played out.

Raider's big bay was in a little better condition than the other horses. When the two groups had approached to within a hundred yards, he urged his horse into a slow canter. So did Jeff. He and Raider met midway between the posse and the horse herd. "What the hell's this?" Raider asked, pointing to the fifteen fresh horses Sheriff Jones was leading.

Jeff shrugged. "I knew that if you made it in time, it would mean you'd ridden your horses into the ground. So I scared up some remounts."

A wide grin caused Raider's moustaches to curl up a little at the ends. "By God," he muttered. "Maybe you ain't such a kid after all."

Jeff thought he was going to burst with pride. Then Raider focused on Sheriff Jones. "Who the hell'd you bring along with the nags?" he asked.

Jeff quickly explained how he'd been forced to go to Jones, and how eager the sheriff was to nail Jamison, both for revenge and for the reward. Raider nodded. "Right. The agency motto. If you cain't appeal t' their sense o' justice, buy 'em."

By then the two groups had come together. There were hurried introductions. Sheriff Jones looked Hume over appraisingly. "So you're Hume. Damned good work you did up there at Hangtown."

Hume shrugged off the compliment. "I've heard good things about you, Jones." Perhaps he meant it, perhaps he was just being diplomatic, but Jeff noticed Jones puff himself up a little with pleasure.

Raider cut into all the congratulations. "Now. Why the hell are we here?"

Jeff quickly told Raider and Hume what he had overheard in the saloon, about the planned robbery and murder of two rich Basque sheepherders. "How much time we got?" Raider asked.

Jeff reverted to looking a little sheepish. "I don't know. Jamison disappeared earlier this afternoon. Sheriff Jones figures he probably went out to his ranch, the place where Logan has been holing up."

An argument followed. Jones was all for waiting until the robbery actually occurred, and then nailing Jamison and Logan in the act. Jeff disagreed violently. "That's wrong. Why give them a chance to kill two totally innocent men?"

Hume was noncommittal, muttering something about no man being truly innocent, but Raider came in on Jeff's side. "Let's go round 'em up. We'll work out the details later, but with this new information about Jamison's place up north, we'll probably be able to crack his operation. Not to mention savin' the skins of two men."

The route to Jamison's ranch lay through Santa Barbara. the posse men elected to ride their flagging mounts that far. When they reached town, they rode straight to the livery stable. The stable owner's eyes popped when he saw Jeff, the kid he'd run off earlier, in the company of such a hardlooking bunch. Jeff did not deign to pay the man any attention at all. While the others were transferring their saddles and other gear to the fresh mounts, Jeff excused himself. "Be back in a minute," he muttered to Raider.

It was more like ten minutes. Then, just as the men were mounting, and the sheriff was cursing Jeff's disappearance, Jeff himself walked into the stable. Sheriff Jones's mouth dropped open. "Well, I'll be damned," he muttered, staring at Jeff.

Raider hid a smile. At least he's learned a little, he thought as he appraised his assistant. The tight charro pants were back on, and those shiny boots, but with much smaller spurs. Jeff was wearing the fringed buckskin jacket, although the trailing fringes had been cut much shorter. The hat had worn in a little, and didn't look quite as ridiculous as before. The twin pearl-handled pistols, with their crossed gun belts, did not look ridiculous at all. Raider figured that the kid was kind of growing into them.

Raider grinned at Jeff. Jeff grinned back. "Let's ride, men," Raider said.

As they left Santa Barbara, the sun was nearing the horizon. It was almost dark by the time they reached Jamison's ranch. Raider stopped the posse just below the crest of a small hill, on the side facing away from the ranch. He, Hume, the sheriff, and Jeff rode up to the crest, and looked over. The ranch yard was about a hundred yards below them. "Looks nice and quiet down there," Raider said softly.

"Yep," Sheriff Jones grunted back.

"Kinda deserted. There's only two horses in the corral."

"I was thinkin' the same," Jones replied. "An' since I know firsthand that Jamison usually keeps eight or ten nags around the place, I figure they must of already rode out."

"But which way?" Hume asked.

"Guess we're gonna have to ride on down an' ask," Raider replied. "There's somebody there. I see smoke comin' out of the chimney."

It wasn't much of a place. There were only a few buildings, most of them unimpressive, the largest being a ramshackle house, the one from which the smoke was coming. Before anyone up on the hill could decide exactly what to do, the front door of the house opened and a man appeared in the doorway. The men on the hill pulled their horses back a little, afraid that they might have been seen or heard. But the man in the doorway scratched his belly lazily, turned to say something to someone inside the house, then walked off in the direction of the outhouse. He did not appear to be armed.

Raider sat his horse for another moment. "One outside," he said. "My guess is one more in the house. Let's make our move while we got 'em separated."

Nobody even bothered to nod, but a moment later all fourteen men had pushed their horses over the top of the hill, down toward the ranch yard. They did not ride fast; instead, they tried to make their approach relatively silent. Two men dismounted, then posted themselves on either side of the front door, their rifles ready. Raider, along with Hume and Jeff, rode over toward the outhouse. Raider looked over at Jeff, whose horse was right in front of the outhouse door. "Watch your ass, kid. A careful man might keep a shotgun inside there."

Jeff paled, and moved his horse to the side. Raider nodded to one of the posse men. The man grinned, unslung his lariat, and began building a loop. A practiced flip of his wrist settled the loop around the outhouse. The posse man snubbed the end of the lariat around his saddle horn, then spurred his horse away.

The outhouse tipped over quite easily, leaving a very surprised man sitting in the open with his pants down around his ankles. He sprang erect, jerking his pants upwards, shouting, "Goddamn it, Bill, if this is your idea of a—"

The man froze as he saw the circle of armed, grim-faced, mounted men spread out in a circle around him. However, his squawk, along with the crash of the falling outhouse, had been heard inside the house. A man pulled open the door and stuck his head outside. "Hal! What the hell's goin' on—?"

The men posted on either side of the door simply grabbed

his shirt and pulled him out through the door. He fell, sprawling onto the ground. Raider rode over to him and dismounted, with his boots practically straddling the man's head. "Is there anyone else in the house?" Raider asked. "Your life might depend on whether or not you tell me the truth."

"Uh, uh, no," the man stammered. He was obviously so stunned that Raider doubted he'd have had the presence of mind to lie. Nevertheless, he detailed two men to search the house. They came back in less than a minute, reporting that the house was indeed empty.

The outhouse man, Hal, was led over to stand with the man from the house, Bill. By now both men had recovered their wits a little. "What the hell do you varmints mean, ridin' in here like this?" Bill demanded. He turned toward the sheriff. "This ain't like you, Jones. When the judge an' the mayor hear what you done—"

Raider stepped in front of Bill, so that their faces were only a few inches apart. What Bill saw in Raider's eyes dried his mouth out so badly that he was no longer able to speak. "I'll ask you this once," Raider said in a low, flat voice. "Where's Jamison and Logan? Which way did they ride?"

Bill worked up a little more spit, swallowed. "I— They ain't here. They—rode out two, three hours ago."

"To murder two sheepherders," Raider finished for him. He saw a moment's shock in Bill's eyes, shock that Raider knew about the robbery, but Bill tried to brazen it out. "I—don't know what the hell you're talkin' about," he rasped.

Raider made no reply, but stood unmoving for several seconds, looking straight into Bill's eyes. For a moment it looked like it might work, that Bill might crack, but there was a sudden stiffening of the man's resolve. "Go fuck yourself, mister."

Raider smiled. The smile was even more unsettling than Raider's direct stare, a mirthless, cold smile. Raider turned toward the man with the lariat. He pointed toward Hal. "Hang that one—over there, under the corral gate."

The words were spoken matter-of-factly, in a calm, steady voice. Raider's entire demeanor was so relaxed, so unthreatening, that Hal was taken by surprise when two men suddenly grabbed hold of him while another quickly tied his arms behind his back. "Hey, wait a minute. I ain't done nothin'. You cain't—"

But Raider had already turned away and was facing Bill again. "We'll hang him first," he said, jerking his chin toward Hal, who was being dragged toward the corral gate. "You can watch him choke. Then, unless you tell me how to find Jamison and Logan, we'll hang you next."

Bill's face was white as a sheet, but he was not broken yet. "You're bluffin' mister," he snarled. "You wouldn't dare. I—"

Raider smiled that awful smile again. "No? Just watch."

The corral gate was about nine feet high, with a strong crossbar over the top. The lariat had already been thrown over the crossbar. Now Hal was dragged to his feet; his legs did not seem to be working. "No! Don't!" he screamed as the lariat's noose was slipped over his head. One of the men tugged on the lariat, tightening the noose. Hal's scream was cut off in the middle.

Raider turned back toward Bill. "One last chance," he said. "Tell us, or he hangs."

Bill was raging by now. "Goddamn, you miserable murderin' devils. When the law—"

Then his eyes fell on Sheriff Jones, who was the law, and one look at that grim face shut him up. He watched dumbly as the free end of the lariat was once again snubbed around a saddle horn. Once the horse was whipped away, Hal would be pulled up off the ground, with the loop tightening around his neck.

It was Hal who broke first. The noose had loosened a little while the other end of the lariat was being tied to the saddle horn. "Wait!" he shouted. "I'll tell ya. I'll tell ya just where they went!"

Hal stood and babbled, his hands still tied behind his back, the noose around his neck. He told them not only the route the bandits had taken, but where they meant to attack the two travelers. "Just a little ways north o' Santa Maria. The trail narrows there. They kin ride in on 'em from the side, then fill 'em full o' lead 'fore they know what hit 'em."

Hal would have babbled on longer, but Raider nodded to one of the men and the noose was removed. Ten minutes later the two horses in the corral had been saddled and bridled, and both Hal and Bill had been securely tied into their saddles. One of the posse men was detailed to take them back to Santa Barbara and make certain they were locked in a cell.

Then it was time to ride. "Too bad," Hume grated, "about them having maybe a two- or three-hour lead. We might not catch 'em in time."

"We can sure as hell try," Raider said, swinging up into the saddle. A moment later the remaining thirteen posse members had ridden out of the ranch yard, heading north.

Jeff found himself riding alongside Raider. "Uh, that thing about hanging those two men without a trial. You wouldn't have really—"

Raider turned a poker face toward Jeff. "Course not," he said equably.

Jeff felt relieved, until he heard one of the men snigger. "Kid has a lot to learn," someone else said half under his breath.

Jeff turned, angry, but could not tell who had spoken. He turned back toward Raider, whose face still showed nothing. What the hell was he to believe?

He said nothing more. Something else was bothering him. It took him a few minutes to figure out what it was. Thirteen men. They were down to thirteen now. The significance of that number—

"But that's not scientific," he muttered to himself. Still, he felt uncomfortable.

CHAPTER SIXTEEN

The posse rode north for nearly two hours along the coast. They were fortunate in having a nearly full moon; its light made traveling easier.

Jeff was fascinated by the sea. The moonlight silvered the backs of the waves before they broke, then, as the water crashed down, phosphorescence shot green fire in every direction. Later, as they rode along the beach for a little while, there was more phosphorescence; the horses' hoofprints glowed eerily for several seconds after they had been imprinted in the sand. Spooky and beautiful. Such a beautiful land. How could it hold all this killing and terror?

At a place called Gaviota, which meant, appropriately, sea gull, the road left the coast, heading up a steep pass into rugged mountains. The higher they climbed, the narrower the trail became. Raider insisted that scouts ride out ahead, in case of ambush. "We ain't followin' Sunday school teachers," he warned the others.

After an hour and a half of hard climbing, they reached a mountainous plateau. The steep grade had been wearing on the horses. "We gotta keep these nags in condition for fightin'," Raider said. "Us too. It might be a good idea to take us a break for a while."

Sheriff Jones did not like the idea. "They'll gain on us," he insisted.

"Mebbe," Raider said drily. "But if they got any brains, they're restin' their horses right now."

Hume threw his weight in on Raider's side, so they stopped for two hours. Most of the men slept. Jeff, sleepless, looked over at Raider, who was apparently out like a light. How could he be so relaxed when the morning would probably bring danger, even death?

By two in the morning they were ready to push on. Raider checked his horse, the remount Sheriff Jones had provided. It was a good animal, but not as good as his bay. He wondered how the horse would behave in a fight, with bullets whistling past, with men and horses screaming, and guns going off near its ears. Well, he'd find out soon enough.

They reached Santa Maria at dawn. It was a small place; they rode right on through. A few miles the other side of town they saw a lone figure approaching from the north. Jeff, with his phenomenal vision, identified him before anyone else: a ragged Mexican farmer, riding a mule.

The Mexican looked a little nervous as the posse closed in around him. Raider spoke to the man in Spanish, politely, which seemed to relax him. Yes, señor, the Mexican reported, several armed men had indeed ridden past him, heading in the same direction as the posse. It had happened just a half hour earlier. Yes, they were all armed. "A strange thing, señor," the Mexican said, lowering his voice. "When they passed by me, each of them pulled their hats down over their faces as if they did not want me to be able to remember who they were."

But the Mexican had seen enough to give descriptions that could easily match Jamison and Logan. Hume pulled Raider aside, out of the Mexican's hearing. "Sounds like they're only about forty-five minutes ahead of us," he said. "Perhaps they rested their horses a little longer than we rested ours."

"Time to push on hard," Raider said, urging his horse into

a fast trot. The posse followed, leaving the Mexican alone on his mule, scratching his head, but happy that he was far from whatever trouble these crazy gringos were planning.

An hour later they began to smell the sea again; it was not far ahead. They had been riding over a hilly plateau. Now the land started to dip toward a shallow pass that would take them to the ocean. Sheriff Jones began to grouse nervously. "I thought the man we almost strung up said Jamison and the others were gonna hit their targets just north of Santa Maria."

"We're north of Santa Maria," Jeff reminded him.

"But it's late—"

Raider shrugged. "Mebbe the men they're gonna rob are movin' kinda slow. Mebbe Jamison and Logan are just settin' somewhere waitin' for 'em t' show up. Which means we better be extra careful, 'cause we could ride into a trap just as easy as those sheepmen."

"Ah hell," Jones murmured. "Back at Jamison's place they told us there was only seven or eight of 'em. If they try an' hit us, we'll—"

Suddenly there was the sound of gunfire, coming from about a quarter mile ahead. "Too late!" Raider shouted. He spurred his horse into a gallop. "Come on, you bastards! Let's go git 'em!"

The posse thundered down into the pass, strung out in a ragged column—too damned spread out for Raider's taste—but they had to get there fast, or they'd find nothing but two dead Basques.

The scene they rode into was not a pretty one. Two men, no doubt the Basques, had been ambushed at a wide spot in the trail. As the posse thundered around the final bend, Raider saw that one of the victims was lying in a pool of blood, so much blood that he was probably already dead. The other man had managed to crawl behind his horse; the animal had been shot. The man was banging away at the bandits with a pistol.

Raider made a quick count of the bandits. There were

seven men still in the saddle, with one on the ground, unless others were hiding somewhere alongside the trail. The downed bandit was sitting, hunched over, holding a hand to his stomach. The cornered Basques had obviously exacted a price.

But the remaining Basque would not survive for long. Two of the bandits were swinging wide in a flanking movement, obviously meaning to get behind him. Raider was pretty sure that one of them was Jamison. It was only then that the bandits became aware of the posse.

The posse hit hard. Raider saw the bandits nearest to him pull their horses back in shock, then posse members and bandits were mingling, no more time for thinking, planning. Using his Winchester, Raider shot a man out of the saddle. Then a bandit was firing at him, from his left. Raider tried to bring his rifle barrel around, but his horse, obviously not used to gunfights, shied, flinging its head so high that Raider could not bring his rifle around to bear. The bandit, his face twisted into a grimace of hatred and triumph, was sighting on Raider again, ready to cut him down.

Blam! A gun went off right next to Raider, and the bandit who'd been about to shoot him was gone, blown right out of his saddle. Raider glanced to his left, and saw Jeff, white-faced, levering another round into the barrel of his Winchester.

The fight had lasted only a few seconds so far, but most of the bandits were either down or running for cover. Raider saw one man race his horse into thick brush. He immediately followed.

Once in the brush, visibility was limited. Where the hell had the bastard gone? Then he saw the tail end of a horse scooting around a big boulder to his left. Cutting to his right, Raider headed for the far side of the boulder, intending to cut off his quarry.

He did cut him off, much too effectively. Raider's untrained mount collided with the horse of the man he was chasing. Both animals reared high. Raider heard a gun go off in front of him. His horse screamed, then went down. Raider barely had time to kick himself free of the stirrups. He hit hard, rolling over and over in an effort to make himself a more difficult target.

But the other man's horse had gone down too, throwing its rider. Raider, scrambling erect, saw the horse getting shakily to his feet, while the man he'd been chasing staggered toward the excited animal, trying to catch the reins. But the horse, neighing in terror, galloped away.

With the horse out of the way, Raider and the other man were suddenly facing one another, about a dozen yards apart. And then they recognized one another.

Logan! It was Logan himself!

If Raider's surprise was considerable, Logan's was much greater. "You!" he hissed, his eyes bulging, as if he'd seen a ghost. Of course, Raider thought, he's been thinking all this time that those two bushwhackers of his killed me.

Both men had lost their rifles, but both were wearing pistols. "It's all over, Logan," Raider shouted. "Give it up."

Raider wanted to take Logan alive, he wanted him as a witness against Jamison, but Logan was not about to surrender. Even as Raider shouted his warning, Logan was reaching for his pistol.

Raider, drawing a split second later, stepped a little to one side. Logan shot first, but his bullet narrowly missed Raider, plucking at the sleeve of his jacket. Raider's bullet did not miss, but took Logan high in the stomach, doubling him up. Logan backpedaled several steps, and might have regained his balance, but Raider shot him again, his next bullet hitting Logan in the chest.

The impact knocked Logan over onto his back. But he still held his pistol. Twisting around on the ground, he tried to cock the hammer, but he could not seem to summon up the strength. Still, he tried, his face twisted with concentration. "Drop it, Logan!" Raider shouted, starting forward.

"The 'ell with that, maittee," Logan snarled, his accent the heaviest Raider had yet heard it. "Damned if I'll hang."

Raider heard the hammer of Logan's forty-five click back into full cock. The barrel swung shakily toward him. Raider had no choice now. His own pistol bucked in his hand. The bullet hit Logan in the throat, knocking him flat. His pistol flew from his hand.

Logan was dead by the time Raider reached him. He stood looking down at the corpse. "Well, there's another Duck who'll never fly again," he murmured.

Meanwhile, Jeff had his hands full. He'd seen Raider ride away after a fleeing bandit. He thought of riding after him, but he had problems of his own to contend with. The main bulk of the bandits were all snarled up with the posse; only the two who'd made the flanking ride around the two Basques were all by themselves. Even as Jeff watched, one of them was knocked from the saddle by a posse man's bullet. The other man screamed a curse at the Basque who had helped foil his plans. Gouging his spurs into his horse's side, he started forward, pistol held high, obviously ready to shoot the man in the back. The Basque was making no move to defend himself; either he was not aware that there was anyone behind him, or, more likely, he was too badly wounded to fight any more. Jeff could see blood on the man's clothing.

Which left only Jeff. He was far out to the side, having ridden right through most of the fighting after shooting down the man who'd tried to kill Raider. Now, it was up to him to save the Basque; and he was scared, because he'd recognized that lone bandit as Meriwether Jamison. A man with a reputation, a proven killer.

Jeff charged anyhow, riding in hard, surprising Jamison so thoroughly that the shot he'd already aimed at the wounded Basque missed. Then, before he could bring his pistol around to bear, Jeff had already opened up with his rifle.

Bullets flew fast and thick. Jamison was firing back, but the range was over fifty yards, and at that range a man with a pistol is at a considerable disadvantage against a man with a rifle. Still, Jamison was a fine shot, and one of his bullets hit

Jeff's horse, but not before Jeff had seen Jamison reel in the saddle. He'd hit him!

However, Jeff's horse was falling, and Jamison, bent forward in the saddle, holding his side, was riding away toward some brush. Jeff wanted to cry out, to tell others to go after Jamison, ride him down, but he was, at the moment, flying through the air. When he hit he was amazed by how hard the ground was; the impact so thoroughly knocked the wind out of him that it was a couple of minutes before he could breathe again, and by then Jamison had vanished into the brush.

There was no more firing. Jeff turned, and saw that the fight was over. A ring of posse men surrounded the three or four bandits left alive. They were a dejected group, all unhorsed by now, huddling together on the ground. Every one of them appeared to be wounded.

Jeff checked his horse. It was alive, but badly wounded. Pulling out his pistol, he shot the animal through the head. It was not an easy thing to do, but by now he seemed to be running more on instinct than on cold calculation.

He turned and started walking back toward the wounded Basque; then he realized that he had not seen Raider among the posse men. He remembered seeing him ride off into the brush after a fleeing bandit. Jeff stood undecided for a moment, wondering whether to help the wounded man in front of him, or go after Raider.

The problem was solved when Raider came limping out of the brush, carrying his rifle and saddle. Jeff saw him stop to talk to Hume. He heard him say, "Logan's dead. Where's Jamison?"

"Don't know," Hume replied. Jeff knew where Jamison was—at least, where he'd gone—but he found that he was having trouble talking. He bent over the wounded man, who looked up at him with a snarl on his face. He saw the Basque's hand tighten around the handle of his pistol. "Take it easy, old timer," Jeff said softly. "We're friends. It's all over now."

The wounded man grunted, then let his pistol drop from

suddenly lax fingers. He was an older man, perhaps in his late fifties. "Juan—my partner," the Basque murmured, trying to turn toward the dead man lying next to him.

"I think he's done for," Jeff said gently. "Let's see about you."

Jeff was aware of someone standing next to him. He looked up. It was Raider and Hume. They both knelt down and helped him roll the Basque over. Jeff was amazed by the amount of blood. "Not too bad," Hume said. "They got him in the shoulder and leg. If he gets good care, he'll live."

Jeff was aware of Raider's eyes on him. "Jamison," Jeff blurted. "He rode off into the brush. I—think I got him in the side."

Raider looked just a little surprised. "Good work," he said.

Raider hesitated for a moment. His expression was inscrutable. "Thank's for savin' my hide back there," he said gruffly. "Nice shootin'."

Jeff didn't know what to say. "Isn't anyone going after Jamison?" he finally blurted.

Hume answered. "Later. We have two men wounded, not to mention this gentleman." He pointed to the wounded Basque, then to the dead one. "And a man who's going to need burying."

Jeff wandered away as more men came to fuss over the wounded Basque. He sat on a rock, staring into space. He looked down at his hands, to see if they were shaking. He was amazed to see that they were not, although he felt as if his entire being was trembling.

A shadow fell on him. He looked up. Raider was looking down at him. "You all right, kid?" Raider asked.

Jeff started to nod, but knew that it would be a lie. "I—don't know," he finally replied. "I—"

He looked up at Raider, agony on his face. "I—I've never shot a man before. Never—killed anyone—"

Raider nodded, his face still inscrutable. "And it bothers you," he said.

Jeff nodded jerkily. "Yes—yes. It bothers the hell out of me."

Raider looked off to the side. Jeff could not see the expression on his face, but he was aware of half-suppressed emotion in Raider's voice. "Good," Raider was saying. " 'Cause if it ever stops botherin' you, you're in big trouble, mister."

CHAPTER SEVENTEEN

The next hour was spent building travois for the wounded and the dead. The surviving Basque insisted on taking his partner back to San Luis Obispo for burial. Even the dead bandits were taken away. Their bodies would be photographed, and the photographs sent to the Chicago main office of the Pinkerton National Detective Agency. Standard policy. Photographs of dead desperadoes were often useful in clearing up old mysteries.

When the work was well underway, Raider transferred all his gear to one of the dead bandits' horses. Jeff did the same. "Now," Raider said. "Show me which way Jamison headed."

Jamison's trail led through dense underbrush. Raider pointed to reddish-brown stains that had been splashed on leaves and stones. "Dried blood," he told Jeff. "Looks like you hit him pretty good. We'll ride slow through here. He may be holed up, hurtin' bad, an' wantin' t' hurt back."

But Jamison was not in the brush. The tracks of his horse led back to the main trail. "He's headin' north," Raider decided. "I wonder why? Lookin' for a doctor, mebbe?"

They pushed on, but not as quickly as Raider would have liked. The bandits' horses, having traveled most of the night, were tired. Of course, Jamison's horse would be in the same condition.

They almost missed the man and the horse hidden in the bushes, but the horse whickered when it heard Jeff's and Raider's mounts passing by. Raider caught a quick glimpse of the animal, its outline nearly obscured by brush. He could also see part of a man's leg, sticking out from under a bush. "Watch yourself!" Raider called out to Jeff, while at the same time jerking his Winchester from its saddle scabbard.

But the leg did not move. Then a weak groan came from the brush, the groan of a man without a lot of fight left in him. "Dismount," Raider told Jeff. "I think Jamison's in there, hurt bad, but he might still be able t' bite back."

Jeff swung down, rifle in hand. "That's his horse, all right," he said, squinting into the brush. Then he took a closer look at what he could see of the leg. "But he was wearing different colored pants."

Nevertheless, both men moved into the brush carefully, rifles cocked and ready. However, they did not find Jamison; they found instead a badly wounded man they had never seen before. He looked up as they approached, his eyes widening in fear when he saw their weapons. "Don't—shoot me again," he moaned.

They quickly convinced him they were there to help. While Raider bound up the wound in the man's side, the man told them that a stranger had stopped him on the road, shot him without warning, then rode off on his horse, leaving his own horse behind. When questioned, the wounded man remembered that his assailant's shirt had been soaked in blood.

"Damn it," Raider muttered. "Now Jamison has a fresh mount, and we're still ridin' these tired out old hay-burners."

The man was too badly hurt to ride, so Raider and Jeff started building another travois. They were just lashing it into place on Jamison's horse, when Hume and the rest of the posse came in sight, leading their own caravan of hurt and misery.

Raider turned the wounded man over to Hume. It was agreed that Hume would continue on to San Luis Obispo, where he would get help for the wounded, then have a warrant issued for Jamison's arrest. "That shot-up Basque got a good look at his face," Hume said grimly. "He'll testify. No crooked prosecutor or judge will get the bastard off this time."

Raider and Jeff pressed on after Jamison, but with little luck. They had reached the coast again. There were small communities near the beach, and with San Luis Obispo only a few miles ahead, the road was well-traveled. There was no sure way to pick out Jamison's tracks among all the others. When they reached San Luis Obispo they questioned several people, but no one remembered seeing a wounded man ride into town.

By then it was growing late. As the light faded, Jeff realized how tired he was. So far, he'd been going on nerves, but as the excitement of the fight and the chase began to fade, so did his energy. Jeff looked over at Raider. He didn't look tired at all. How did he do it? Maybe he'd only learned to hide it, because, to Jeff's relief, Raider suggested they turn in for the night. "Tired eyes can miss tracks rested eyes would see in a moment," he explained.

They slept in beds that night; Jeff was in no mood for hard ground. They were up at dawn. Raider conferred with Hume for a few minutes, then he and Jeff headed back along the trail, toward Santa Maria.

"Watch the edges of the trail," Raider said to Jeff. "We got two possibilities: either the son of a bitch swung wide around San Luis Obispo and kept on goin' north, or he slipped off to the side into the brush. He may be hidin' anywhere. Hell, with that bullet you put in him, he may even be dead. Keep an eye cocked for buzzards."

It was Jeff who found the place where Jamison had left the main trail. At first the tracks didn't register, then he saw a faint line of hoofprints branching off to the right. "Raider!" he called out.

They followed the tracks cautiously; the brush was thick here, they could ride right up to a cornered man before they saw him. But they found no one, just some trampled grass where someone had sat down in a small cleared space for a while. Raider dismounted, his eyes tracking over the ground. "Look at this," he said. Jeff looked. There were small scraps of bloody cloth. "It's Jamison all right," Raider said. "He bandaged his wound here. He may not be hurt as bad as I thought."

Jamison had mounted again, and ridden away through the brush. They followed his tracks in a big circle back to the main trail, where the tracks turned south. Raider spat on the ground in disgust. "The bastard just sat there and waited for us to go on by," he muttered. "I'll betcha a wooden nickel he's headed back toward Santa Barbara. Home ground."

Realizing how much of a lead Jamison had over them, they pushed on as fast as they could, although they had to be careful that Jamison pulled no more tricks, like branching off the trail again. They rode until dark, then bedded down for the night, afraid of missing one of Jamison's ploys in the darkness. By noon the next day they were in Santa Barbara. They headed straight for the jail. The two men they'd captured three days earlier, at Jamison's ranch, were still in their cells. Sheriff Jones's deputy assured them that no one had reported any sightings of Jamison in the area.

Raider left the jail in a bad mood. "That half-wit's too damned lazy an' stupid t' keep his eyes open. I'll bet Jamison's here somewhere."

They asked questions around town, but received mostly sullen replies. Jamison still had his adherents in Santa Barbara. It was not until Hume and Sheriff Jones rode in the next day, armed with warrants, and the full story of Jamison's depredations, that public opinion began to change. "There's a lotta folks 'round here," Sheriff Jones said, grinning evilly, "that got burned real bad by those robberies Jamison set up. Yesterday he was a golden boy, today ever'body wants his blood."

However, there was still no sign of Jamison. The big break came on the fourth day. Raider and Jeff were in the sheriff's office. Raider was playing gin rummy with the sheriff when they heard shouting outside. A moment later a bedraggled man with a cut on his cheek staggered in through the door. Sheriff Jones jumped up from his desk. "Why, Doctor Quimby," he said. "You look like you got run over by a herd o' longhorns. What the hell happened?"

"Plenty," Quimby snarled. He proceeded to recount an interesting tale. Two nights before, two men had come to his house and taken him away at gunpoint. He'd been led, blind-folded, to a house in a remote location. "That damned black-guard, Jamison, was there," Quimby snarled. "Had a bullet in his side. Ordered me to take it out. *Ordered* me, Goddamn it, like I was some kinda servant, like I wouldn't of taken it out if he'd asked me nice."

"How bad was he hurt?" Raider interjected.

Quimby shrugged. "He won't move too fast for a while, but he'll live."

Quimby's face changed from angry to grim. "After I took the bullet out, they locked me up in a storage room. Full of rats. They didn't think I could hear 'em talkin' but I could. The men who'd grabbed me and took me out to the house wanted to let me go in a day or two, but Jamison, the son of a bitch, said they'd have to kill me, or I'd talk. Damn! To think of all the nice things I did for that man in the past."

The doctor shook his head hard. "Anyhow, I dug my way out through an adobe wall. Took off at dawn. I been runnin' and hidin' half the day. I could hear 'em lookin' for me."

"I suppose you could find the place again," Raider said.

Doctor Quimby nodded his head vigorously. "You bet your ass. Just give me a gun and I'll lead the way. I'll blow that damned snake halfway to Kansas."

It took the sheriff a half hour to round up a twenty-man posse. "Now they all want his blood," Raider observed. "A week ago, the man could do no wrong."

The place where the doctor had been held captive was in the hills, about ten miles back of town. The posse stopped on a small ridge overlooking it. There was only one building, an old adobe hacienda, much run down. Raider could believe the doctor's story about the rats.

None among them had expected to find anyone there. Before they'd left town, Raider had said to the sheriff, "After Quimby escaped, I'll bet they all lit out like their tails were on fire."

He was surprised, then, to see evidence of occupation below. Smoke rose from a sagging stovepipe. Several horses contentedly munched hay in a ramshackle corral. There were also signs of imminent departure; a wagon stood close to the front door. It was packed with gear. "We made it just in time," Sheriff Jones said, satisfaction all over his face. Raider figured he must be thinking about the reward.

As they watched, a man started out the front door with his arms full of belongings. Before Raider knew what he was about to do, the sheriff sang out loudly, "You! You down there! Drop what you got in your hands an' raise 'em high!"

Naturally, the man, after one stunned look up toward the twenty horsemen sitting on the skyline, dropped his armful and ducked back inside the house, slamming the door behind him. Raider swore silently. If Jones had kept his big mouth shut, they could have easily surrounded the place, maybe even taken Jamison and the others prisoners without a fight.

Everyone in the posse heard a tinkle of broken glass from below. A moment later a rifle barrel poked out through a window. "Back!" Raider shouted.

Horsemen scrambled this way and that. The rifle bellowed. One of the posse men yelled as a bullet nicked his ear. His yell propelled the other men into increasingly frantic action. Within seconds, all twenty men were safely on the far side of the hill, screened from the house below.

Raider and Jeff sat their horses off to one side, watching as Sheriff Jones deployed his men around the house. "Not even a mouse is gonna get out of there alive," Jones boasted to Raider.

As he bustled off, Raider said to Jeff, out of the side of his mouth, "Trouble is, we ain't after mice. Damn! This is gonna get messy."

It did. First, the sheriff identified himself, then once again ordered everyone inside the house to come out with their hands up. "Go away," someone cried out from the house. "We ain't done nothin'."

"Prove it by throwin' out your guns," the sheriff bellowed back."

"Fuck you, sheriff!"

Once again a rifle barrel was thrust out through the broken window. Once again it roared, this time plucking Sheriff Jones's hat from his head. "Jesus H. Christ!" the sheriff shouted, ducking back behind cover, his face white. "That bastard can shoot. Well, so can we."

Under the sheriff's orders, the posse opened up a whithering fire on the house. Tiles flew off the roof, what little window glass there was quickly disappeared, splinters flew from the wooden veranda, but nothing of any real importance was accomplished. It was an adobe house, and the thick earthen walls soaked up lead quite handily. From time to time the defenders stuck rifles out through the windows and shot back, but for the most part, they were content to keep their heads down. The siege might have gone on for days, had not Raider, a little after four o'clock, decided he'd had enough.

The house was pretty much one room, with the little store-room where Quimby had been imprisoned jutting out a few feet from the back wall. The only way for bullets to get inside, where the defenders were holed up, was through the door, and through two small windows. That left a couple of corners where the defenders could huddle, safe from bullets. What was needed was a way to increase the field of fire inside the building.

Raider had noticed that two of the posse men had large-bore buffalo rifles, like his own. He pulled his Sharps from its scabbard, then motioned for the men to come with him.

Positioning the men on either side of himself, Raider began firing at a point in the adobe wall, shot after shot. The other

men did the same. It took a while, but eventually the huge
slugs dug a hole right through the wall, not a large hole, but a
hole wide enough for men with rifles of lesser caliber to start
spraying lead into areas hitherto inaccessible.

With one hole made, Raider moved to the other side of the
building. Once again, it took a while, but now there was
another wall with a hole in it—and no place left to hide.

It was only a half hour more before the men inside gave
up. Just as it was beginning to grow dark, there was movement at one of the windows, and a moment later a dirty white
shirt was seen fluttering from the end of a broom handle.
Rifles roared. The broom stick was splintered. "Hold your
fire, you idiot jackasses!" Raider shouted. "They're tryin' t'
give up." One more rifle went off. Then, under Raider's
glare, silence fell.

A few seconds later a scared voice floated up to them. "No
more shootin'—please. Jeb's hit bad, an' my arm don't
work no more."

"Come out the front door," Raider ordered. "One at a time."

A moment's hesitation. "I'll hafta drag Jeb," the voice
called out.

"Then drag him."

There wasn't much more than hinges left of the door. A
moment later Raider saw movement just inside the doorway.
A man appeared, bent over, dragging another man behind
him. The posse waited until the two men were several yards
from the doorway, then they closed in from both sides.
Sheriff Jones pushed by the man doing the dragging. He
looked down at the wounded man. "Damn!" he burst out.
"That's not Jamison!"

He spun toward the other prisoner. "Where's Jamison?"
he rasped. "Is he still in there? Dead, maybe?"

The man who'd surrendered shook his head in confusion.
"Jamison?" he asked. "Is he why you're here?"

"You bet your boots, mister."

The man's shoulders slumped. "I wish you woulda told us
that right off, sheriff. Jamison ain't here. He lit out for Los
Angeles a little after dawn."

CHAPTER EIGHTEEN

Raider considered starting after Jamison himself, and sending Jeff back to inform Hume. Then he reconsidered. Maybe it wouldn't be such a bad idea to have some help along. He looked appraisingly at Jeff, who was helping bandage the wounded. He'd done a damned good job of setting up Jamison, and later, of providing remounts for the posse. And then there was that little incident when the kid had saved Raider's life, the morning they'd jumped Jamison and Logan north of Santa Maria. Maybe it wouldn't be such a bad idea to take Jeff along after all.

Raider walked over to Jeff. "You ready t' ride, kid?" he asked.

Jeff looked up, a big smile creasing his features. "After Jamison? Sure."

Raider wrote out a note for the sheriff to send on to Hume. He hoped it would get there; the sheriff was grumpy. They'd failed to get Jamison; there would be no reward this time.

Raider and Jeff rode out an hour later. Dusk caught them at Ventura. To Jeff's delight, Raider elected to set up camp on the beach, just a few yards from the high tide line. After they'd eaten, Raider lay on his bedroll, watching the sunset turn the horizon into a kaleidoscope of reds, pinks, and yellows, while Jeff skipped stones over the water. Amazing how soothing the sound of the surf was. Yep. Damned if he might not decide to settle here some day, if he ever got old enough to think seriously about settling down.

The next morning Raider elected to turn inland, rather than ride straight down the coast. "Is it shorter this way?" Jeff asked.

Raider shrugged. "Mebbe a little. Truth is, I got some friends t' see along the way."

A few miles farther along, the trail branched. The left branch headed back toward Newhall, and Logan's New South Wales Inn. Raider took the right branch, which led toward a rugged wall of mountains about ten miles ahead. There was a pass through those mountains that led toward Los Angeles. At the head of that pass lay Calabasas.

They reached Banks's settlement late in the afternoon. The nervousness of the guards indicated to Raider that things were not going well. "More bushwhackins'," Banks told him lugubriously. "That crazy son of a bitch, Leonis, got two more of my men."

Though Raider and Jeff spent the night in the settlement, Banks didn't waste any energy trying to convince Raider to stay. "We ain't gonna be driven off," Banks said the next morning, when the two Pinkertons were already mounted and ready to ride off. "If I leave, it'll be feet first."

Raider nodded, but said nothing. In a way, there was not that much difference between Leonis and Banks. Both were squatting on land that belonged to the government, land that had once belonged to the Spaniards who'd colonized the area, and before them, to the Indians. Both men were willing to kill for the land, probably both were willing to die for it, too, something that Raider could not understand. If land became crowded, or difficult to hold, why not just travel on and find a better place?

The two Pinkertons rode on. Jeff had asked few questions while they were at Banks's place. As they rode, Raider filled him in on the situation. Jeff, an admirer of order and rationality, was appalled. "Can't the law—?" he started to ask.

"Forgit the law in these parts," Raider replied grimly. "There ain't that much of it around, besides us."

They rode warily. Raider knew that if Leonis spotted him, life could become very interesting. Maybe even very short. However, they came through the mountains unmolested. The far side of the pass led down into a huge, dry, brushy valley. Halfway across the valley they turned south, into Sepulveda Pass. Once across the pass, the vastness of the Los Angeles basin lay before them, miles and miles of mostly empty brush- and tree-covered land. In the distance they could barely make out a dense layer of haze, lying over the sea. Turning east, they rode along the base of brush-covered hills.

They reached Los Angeles late in the afternoon. "Not much of a place, is it?" Jeff said as they rode into the town's little plaza. Most of the buildings were of adobe; long, low structures with flat roofs. There were a few modern buildings, but not a hell of a lot to show after nearly thirty years of Yankee occupation. Raider and Jeff checked into one of the newer hotels, a big frame structure that looked out of place among the adobes.

After they'd cleaned off a little trail dirt, Raider and Jeff asked the hotel clerk where they could find Juan Mascarel. "Oh, the mayor?" the clerk asked. "Course, he ain't been mayor for a while, but he's still around. Lives over in Sonora Town."

Banks had suggested that Raider look up Mascarel as soon as he got to Los Angeles. "He's a Frenchman," Banks had told him. "He's a good man, which makes me wonder how he ever got elected mayor. He can tell you a lot about Los Angeles."

They found Mascarel's house, a squat adobe near the edge of town. When they knocked, a woman's voice replied, "Entra . . . Entra!" Jeff pushed open the door, then stopped so abruptly that Raider almost ran into him. "Uh, sorry ma'am," Jeff stammered. "We didn't mean to—"

An Indian woman, perhaps forty years old, was seated on the dirt floor, grinding corn in a stone *metate*. She was naked to the waist. She looked up at Jeff with a total lack of concern. After quickly appraising the two men, she turned just her head, and called out, "Juan."

A lean, rather tired-looking man entered the room. "Yes?" he said, looking from Jeff to Raider.

Raider quickly introduced himself and Jeff, then told Mascarel that they had been sent by Banks. At the mention of Banks's name, Mascarel became all affability. He extended his hand, then nodded toward the Indian woman. "My wife," he said. She did not look up again, but continued her grinding, her rather pendulous breasts swaying back and forth.

Mascarel led them to a small internal patio. It was a very pleasant place, with a little garden of shrubs and flowers. It was made even more pleasant when Mascarel produced a bottle of wine. Food followed, the Indian woman bringing in plates full of tortillas, meat, and beans, accompanied by the inevitable fierce chili sauce. Even Jeff had to admit that the tortillas were delicious. All that grinding obviously paid off.

The talk turned to Los Angeles. "A difficult place," Mascarel told them. "During the fifties, it was a paradise. The local landowners, most of them of Spanish descent—they still had their huge ranchos—made a lot of money by selling beef to the gold camps up north. Then there was a terrible drought which killed most of the cattle. After that came a disaster worse than locusts, one of the great plagues of civilization: the money lenders. The poor Spanish, they had no idea at all of modern business. Even with their herds and land, they had little cash. Imagine how happy they were when they found nice friendly men who would give money to them in exchange for signing a little piece of paper. And oh, the interest, how it mounted up. Then, after the drought, with no cattle left to sell, the Spanish, the old order, they lost their land to those little pieces of paper.

"Then, your terrible war began, after Lincoln was elected. The good men went back east to fight, and the town filled up with scum from the South, men who talked big but who didn't seem eager to rush back home to risk their necks.

They're still here: gamblers, thieves, killers, trash. There are enough of them to elect mayors, sheriffs, and prosecutors. I am a little embarrassed, messieurs, to have numbered myself among that herd of official thieves and assassins.''

Mascarel waved a hand around his modest abode. "You see that my former eminence has not brought me much worldly gain. I was sickened a few years ago, when the mob murdered most of our local Chinese. Ah, what a night that was; screams, shots, cries for mercy, but there was no mercy to be found. For a few weeks after the massacre there was a movement to see the perpetrators of that atrocity punished, but in the end, they only hanged a few innocent Mexicans, men with no one among the powerful to help them.''

Mascarel fell silent for a moment, during which he uncorked another bottle of wine. "Yes, a strange place, our Los Angeles," he murmured. "It has a terrible attraction for the worst sort of men, even this place where I live, Sonora Town. It's named for the people who live here, Mexicans who arrived after the Yankees came. The worst kind of Mexican, from Sonora, the kind of men who would never have been allowed inside California when it was a part of Mexico.''

As for Meriwether Jamison, Mascarel knew nothing about him, except that Los Angeles would be a fine place for him to hide out. "Watch yourself," Mascarel warned. "If he has money, he will have protectors. Powerful protectors.''

Later, on the way back to the hotel, a little heavy-headed from the wine, Jeff complained. "It sounds like we're wasting our time here. Can't we call in some outside help?''

"Sure," Raider replied. "We could bring in a lot of men. Then Jamison would just ride on out, if he's actually here; maybe ride on down into Mexico. But don't forget; we got one thing goin' for us. Jamison's hurt. You put a hole in him. Accordin' to that doctor he shanghaied, he'll want to take some time to build up his strength. Which is why I think he's prob'ly here somewhere, holed up.''

Jeff shook his head in exasperation. "But, without a lot of help, how do we find him?''

Raider smiled, a slow, lazy smile. Jeff had seen him smile like that before. It usually meant that somebody was about to land in a lot of trouble. "Maybe we don't find him," Raider replied. "Maybe we'll fix it so that he comes t' us."

CHAPTER NINETEEN

The sheriff of Los Angeles County was a large, florid man who wore a perpetual scowl. "You say you're from the Pinkerton National Detective Agency?" he asked—snorted, actually—the disdain clear in his voice.

"Right," Raider said coolly. "We're after a murderer an' highwayman, Meriwether Jamison, from up Santa Barbara way. We have a warrant for his arrest."

Raider pulled a piece of folded paper from his vest pocket and tossed it onto the sheriff's desk. The sheriff looked at the paper as if it were a tarantula. Finally, he picked it up, perused it, then tossed it back to Raider. "Bullshit," the sheriff said, snorting again. "I've known Jamison for years. He's as fine and upstanding a man as you could hope to find in these parts."

Raider leaned back in his chair. He'd taken a seat even though the sheriff had not offered him one. "Then I'd say these parts have serious troubles," he finally replied. "Jamison's been masterminding a holdup ring that's robbed an' killed from Newhall t' San Luis Obispo."

The sheriff scowled. "That may be the case in Newhall and San Luis Obispo," he said icily. "Although I'm not saying it is. But around here, Meriwether Jamison is a man of some standing. We're not about to sell him out to the

Goddamned Pinkertons. If anybody is gonna have trouble in my county, it's the Pinkerton National Detective Agency. I've got no use for people like you at all.''

Raider met the sheriff's glare steadily. "The feelin's mutual, sheriff.''

The sheriff flushed. He abruptly stood up behind his desk. "I'll give you some free advice, mister Pinkerton man. Take this kid,''—he motioned toward Jeff, which made Jeff flush with anger—"get on your horses, and ride on out of my county. Because if I find you harassing the good people here in my jurisdiction, I'll plant you six feet under.''

Now Raider stood up too. He appeared relaxed, but his eyes pinned the sheriff's eyes. "If you come after me, sheriff,'' he said coolly, "that tin star won't help you one little bit. I'll kill you on the spot.''

Raider did not speak harshly, but the steadiness of his voice, plus the ice in his eyes, made the sheriff turn pale. "You—you get out of here,'' he finally hissed. "Get right on out of my county.''

Raider turned and started toward the door. Jeff followed, but almost bumped into Raider when he stopped and turned back to face the sheriff. "I'm findin' Jamison,'' Raider said. "I'm bringin' that back-shootin', murderin' thief to where the courts an' the hangman can take care o' him. An' I'll tell you agin, sheriff: this is too big a thing for a two-bit Judas like you to stop.''

He walked out of the office, with Jeff a couple of yards behind. Jeff turned back once, and saw the sheriff still standing behind his desk, leaning on his knuckles. His face was white with—with what? Anger? Fear?

Jeff caught up to Raider, who was walking along the street as if nothing out of the ordinary had happened, as if he had not just told an officer of the law that he would kill him if he got in the way. "But why did we go see the sheriff at all?'' Jeff demanded. "Mascarel already told us he's as crooked as a dog's hind leg. He'll probably just warn every hard case in the area that we're—''

"Exactly," Raider said curtly. Then he led the way back to their hotel. They'd gone straight to the sheriff's office after leaving Mascarel's adobe. It was now fully dark. Jeff followed, wanting to ask more questions, but he doubted that Raider wanted to talk. He'd learned enough about him by now to know when to keep quiet. He realized that, despite Raider's cool manner, the conversation with the sheriff had angered him. It had angered Jeff too; he did not like to see corruption in men who were supposed to be society's protectors. But for God's sake—you didn't go around shooting sheriffs!

Jeff did not sleep well that night. He got up early, but saw that the door to Raider's room was still shut. He fretted for the next several hours, passing time cleaning his guns and other gear. Finally, about two in the afternoon, he heard the door to Raider's room open. A moment later there was a knock on his own door. He opened it, to find Raider standing in the hallway, nearly smiling. "Let's go outside," he said. "Get us some food, an' mebbe do a little more advertisin'."

"Advertising?" Jeff asked, perplexed, but Raider was already heading down the hall. Jeff stuffed his forty-fives into their holsters, and followed.

It was hot outside. Every time a horse or wagon passed by, dust rose from the dirty street. More dust would have risen had it not been held down by abundant horse urine and droppings. No one seemed interested in cleaning up the mess.

Farther down the street, a man went by carrying a rifle. Otherwise, not much moved; the afternoon heat had driven most of the citizens inside. The only real signs of life were coming from saloons, which lined both sides of the street. Jeff could hear pianos tinkling, whores laughing, men bawling out curses and jokes. As they passed one saloon, they saw a man lounging in the doorway. The man saw them at about the same time. For a minute his booze-reddened eyes tracked over them, then snapped back. "Hey!" he shouted, turning to face into the saloon. "It's them two Pinks. They're walkin' along the street just as bold as brass."

Apparently the sheriff already had the word out. There was a thunder of boot heels against a wooden floor from inside the saloon, and a moment later a half dozen men crowded into the doorway. Dirty, mean-looking men. "Goddamn," one snarled. "What say we light into 'em, boys. Horsewhip 'em out o' town."

Raider turned his head and studied the men. "You look at them too," he told Jeff. "Remember their faces. Be able t' pick any of 'em out."

"But hadn't we better—?" Jeff asked nervously. All six of the men were armed. All looked terribly dangerous.

"Naw," Raider said curtly. "They ain't drunk enough yet t' have worked up any real courage. Just keep on walkin'."

The two Pinkertons walked along together, Raider obviously lost in thought. Finally his eyes lit up and he started walking faster. "Start lookin' for a hardware store," he told Jeff.

"But—why?"

Raider grinned. "Those yahoos said they was gonna horsewhip us outta town. We oughta help 'em a little by buyin' 'em a horsewhip."

They found a hardware store in a side street. Raider led the way in, then spent ten minutes going over the store's selection of horsewhips and quirts. He finally picked out the nastiest-looking of the lot, one that had a handle loaded with lead shot, and some of the nastiest leather thongs Jeff had ever seen. He shuddered when he thought of being whipped by such an awful engine of destruction.

They went back out into the street. It was cooling down a little. "Keep those sharp eyes o' yours peeled," Raider said. "The moment you catch sight o' one o' those yahoos—"

But Jeff had already seen one. "Over there," he hissed. Indeed, the man who'd first spotted them from the saloon doorway was walking unsteadily along the side of the street, apparently having imbibed a little too much rotgut. Raider immediately crossed the street and headed toward the man, who did not see him until Raider was only a yard or two away. "So, you're gonna run me outta town," Raider said coolly.

The man's eyes bulged with surprise, even with a little fear. Snarling, he reached for his pistol, but Raider brought the lead-loaded handle of the quirt down against the man's wrist. It was a short, chopping blow; Jeff was sure that he could hear bones breaking. The man howled, clutching at his injured wrist, while the pistol fell from his hand.

And then Raider whipped him, beat him mercilessly, cut strips of skin from his face and body, until Jeff thought he was going to be sick. Raider's whip arm finally stopped rising and falling. By then, his victim was lying on the ground, in a pile of horse dung, whimpering with pain and shock. "You're just a bug," Raider said to the man, loudly enough so that he could be heard for quite a distance. By now a small crowd had gathered to see the show. "Just a bug," he repeated. "Meriwether Jamison's the man I'm after. And I mean t' have him."

Leaving the man lying where he'd fallen, Raider continued down the street. They had not gone a block before he and Jeff spotted another of the men from the saloon. The scenario went pretty much as before, with the surprised man beaten to the ground before he could do much to defend himself. Once again, while the injured man cringed on the ground, Raider spoke Jamison's name, and his determination to find him.

A third man met the same fate ten minutes later. Jeff wondered if this was going to keep on all day, if they were simply going to patrol the streets until Raider had horse-whipped all six men. Then suddenly Raider pulled him into the mouth of an alley. "Fun's over," Raider said.

"What?"

Raider pointed down the street, toward the doorway to the saloon where it had all started. Jeff saw a bloody, bedraggled figure staggering in through the doorway. It was the first man Raider had whipped.

"They'll stick t'gether now," Raider said. "The three of 'em that are still in one piece. They'll come gunnin' for us."

Jeff felt a little shiver of fear, mixed with excitement. "Well—" he said, running his fingertips over the butts of his pistols. "It's only three against two now. We—"

"Uh-uh. I don't want any shootin'. That'd give the sheriff a chance t' git up a posse 'gainst us. We'll just do the same as we been doin'."

"But—"

"Uh-uh. No buts. Look. There they are now."

Sure enough, three angry men were coming out through the saloon doors, hitching up their gun belts, shooting fierce glances up and down the street like hunting dogs. To Jeff, they looked dangerous as hell. "Okay," he heard Raider say. "You be the decoy."

"I—what?"

"Come on, quit jawin'. Just walk on down the street like you're on your way t' Sunday school."

Before Jeff could protest further, Raider had shoved him out into the street. Jeff hesitated a moment, aware of how nice a target he made. He heard a shout coming from the direction of the saloon. Looking up, he saw one of the three men pointing toward him. Suddenly, all three were heading in his direction.

Like Sunday school, Jeff thought as he did an abrupt about face and headed off down the street. But he had never hurried on his way to Sunday school the way he was hurrying now. He heard boot heels pounding along after him. He kept expecting the horrible impact of a bullet plowing into his back. But none came. The men wanted to stop him, and look into his eyes as they shot him down. They were so intent on catching up to him that they did not look into the alleyway at all as they passed by. Which made it quite easy for Raider to step out just behind them, and begin using that terrible whip again.

Within seconds, all three men were on the ground, nursing split skulls or broken limbs. Two had tried to draw, but Raider had kicked their guns away into the street. He lashed them with the whip until they howled for mercy, and when they were sufficiently cowed, he finally let his whip arm drop. Once again a sizable crowd had gathered. Apparently the Los Angeles public liked a good show. "The next man who comes after me," Raider said in a loud, clear voice, heard by all, "will git a bullet in his guts. Understood?"

There were no answers from the latest victims. Raider turned his back and started to walk away, then he turned to face them once again, as if just remembering something. "You tell that t' Meriwether Jamison," he snarled. He turned to face the crowd. "Every mother's son o' you tell it t' him."

As Jeff ran to catch up with Raider, he could hear a buzz of conversation coming from the crowd, larded with references to "Jamison," and, "those Pinkertons."

Raider was walking along with considerable speed. Jeff was a little winded when he caught up to him. Drawing alongside, he expected to see a grim look on Raider's face, a look that would match his tone of voice when he'd addressed the crowd. Instead, Jeff was amazed to see Raider fighting to suppress a grin. "What the hell have you been trying to do?" Jeff asked in exasperation.

Now the grin was unmistakable. "I told you afore," Raider said. "It's advertisin'. Plain an' simple advertisin', one o' the greatest inventions o' the nineteenth century."

CHAPTER TWENTY

The advertising paid off three days later. Raider and Jeff were leaving their hotel for breakfast when a ragged Mexican approached and furtively slipped a note into Raider's hand. "Who—?" Raider started to say, but the Mexican had already faded away as fluidly as he had appeared. Raider made no attempt to read the note immediately, but put it in his pocket. Only after he and Jeff were seated, about to order breakfast, did Raider take out the note and look at it. "It's from Mascarel," he told Jeff. "He says a local Mexican knows where Jamison is hidin' out."

"Where?" Jeff asked excitedly.

"We have t' ask the Mexican, after we bail him outta jail."

Although Jeff was eager to head for the jail, Raider insisted on finishing his breakfast: eggs scrambled in the Mexican style, with lots of chili and onions. Only when he had soaked his final tortilla in the last of the juice did Raider consent to leave. "After all," he insisted, "if the bugger's in jail, he ain't goin' nowhere."

But the Mexican they were looking for was no longer in jail; he was already in court. The charge was public drunkenness and disturbing the peace. He stood before the judge, a small, wiry man, looking very dejected, head down, fidgeting with a worn-out old hat.

The judge was a far more interesting specimen, a middle-aged man of Spanish descent, well-dressed, but exuding an air of mild dissipation. The Mexican was quickly found guilty. Sentencing took longer. Raider and Jeff watched as the judge took some notes from his pockets, perused them, then said, sonorously, "Juan Batista, you will pay a fine of forty-nine dollars, or spend forty-nine days in jail."

Juan cringed; obviously, forty-nine dollars was way beyond his means. "Of course," the judge continued, "if you don't have the money, maybe you have something you could trade—"

"I'll cover the forty-nine dollars," Raider sang out. The judge looked up in surprise, which turned to a happy smile when Raider reached into his pocket and pulled out a bundle of bank notes. Since no bailiff came forward to take the money, Raider was about to hand it to the judge himself, when the judge interrupted him. "No. Give it to him."

Raider turned. A seedy man who had been watching the proceedings got up, approached Raider, and held out his hand. Raider gave him the money, which the man counted rather furtively before cramming it into his pocket and leaving the room. "Case dismissed," Raider heard the judge intone behind him. Juan was already heading for the door, so Raider followed him, Jeff at his heels.

They caught up with Juan outside. "I am not try to run away from you, señores," he said, panting a little. "I joos want to get out of there before the judge, he change his mind and ask for more dinero."

"I was wonderin' 'bout the money," Raider replied. "Why forty-nine dollars exactly? And why did I have to give it to that other yahoo?"

"Because," Juan answered, "the judge, he is a good man, but a bad gambler, and he love to gamble, so he lose. Every night. The next day, he joos make a fine to pay his gambling debts. He owe that man forty-nine dollar. I am so glad he did not owe him a hundred. Aren't you?"

Raider threw back his head and laughed, but Jeff was

incensed. "This place," he fumed. "This Los Angeles. It's a national disgrace."

Raider was still chuckling. "You wanna see a national disgrace, kid, visit Washington."

However, business was at hand, and Juan was trying to slip away into an alley. Raider fell in next to him. "It's 'bout time you gave us forty-nine dollars worth of information, hombre. I want to know where Jamison is."

Juan cringed. "Shhhhh. Don' talk so loud, señor. I do not want to die. Here. We moss get off the street."

He was already heading further into the alley. Jeff was about to follow, but Raider laid a hand on his arm. "Careful, kid, it could be a trap.

Juan had stopped a few yards inside the alley. Raider and Jeff stood a few yards from him, both men studying the depths of the alley, with their hands on the butts of their revolvers. Juan smiled for the first time. "I do not cheat you, señores. You want to know where this man, this very bad man, Jamison, is. I am very happy to tell you. He is with the El Monte gang, about fifteen miles from here."

He then went on to tell them how to get to the place where Jamison was hiding. "But take an army with you, señores," he warned. "Those El Monte boys are ver' bad hombres, and Jamison, he is worse than all of them. He beat me, señor, and took my woman. Which is why I want to see him dead."

He looked at Raider hopefully. "You will kill him, won't you?"

"Either that, or we'll see him hang."

Juan seemed satisfied. "Very good, señores. Now, I think it will be good for my health to go visit my cousin in San Diego, until this *cabron*, Jamison, is no more."

Juan melted away down the alley. Raider made no attempt to stop him. "He's either lyin', or he's told us all he knows," he said to Jeff.

Jeff was quite excited. "What do we do now? Call Hume and get some men down here?"

"Sure, after we check out Juan's story. Come on. We're headin' for El Monte."

To make it appear that they were leaving for good, they checked out of the hotel, then rode out of town with all their gear on their horses. Raider had made a few oblique references to San Diego when leaving the hotel, so they headed south for a while. Only when they were several miles from town did they finally turn east, in the direction of El Monte.

The location Juan had given them was not in El Monte itself, but up in the foothills of the rugged San Gabriel range that loomed to the north. California was a land of mountains. They were everywhere; huge, wild, impassable in places, full of hideouts for men on the run.

They rode carefully, keeping off main trails, which slowed them considerably; it was late in the afternoon before they began to near their goal. "Juan didn't give too good directions, did he?" Raider mused, studying the landscape. They were at the base of the mountains now. Several rugged canyons lay ahead. But which one was the canyon Juan had described? "Tell you what," Raider said. "You take that one on the right, I'll head up the one on the left. Remember what Juan said. There'll be an old adobe ruin about half a mile up the canyon we're lookin' for."

They split up. Raider sat his horse for a few minutes, watching Jeff ride away. A few weeks ago he wouldn't have trusted the kid out of his sight. Now, well, damn, he was shaping up.

Turning his horse, Raider rode up the left-hand canyon. He figured he'd ride maybe a mile. If he found nothing, he'd head back to see if Jeff had had better luck.

However, he'd only gone half a mile when there it was, an old abandoned adobe. A closer view would tell him if it was the right one; Juan had said that there was a grave about fifty yards behind the adobe, with a stone cross.

Raider was only twenty-five yards from the adobe when he had his first inkling that maybe it wasn't abandoned after all. A horse whinnied from behind some brush. He was reaching for his Winchester when a voice froze him in place. "Do not move, señor, or you will be full of holes."

The voice had come from behind and to Raider's left. He was considering making a break for it, when he heard rifles being cocked to his right. Damned if he hadn't gotten himself surrounded.

Slowly turning his head, Raider saw three men covering him from the right. Two more were stepping out of the adobe ahead of him, while a man stood to his left, grinning from ear to ear. "Welcome, señor," the man said, grinning even wider. "It is seldom that anyone comes up here." He laughed, showing bad teeth. "It is even less often that they leave."

The man was big, unkempt, and he had Sonora bandit written all over him: the enormous sombrero, the huge drooping moustaches, the crossed cartridge belts, and the twin pearl-handled revolvers.

He came all the way out into the open. Raider noticed that the bandit speaking was the only one who was not pointing a gun at him. All the others were; he was presently covered by five rifles, held by men that were every bit as threatening as the man with the pearl-handled revolvers, but much more ragged.

The big man came closer, grinning. "Allow me to introduce myself, señor. I am Andres Navares. You are in my valley. Why?"

Navares was still grinning, but his tone was not amused. "I'm lookin' for a man that did me some dirt," Raider replied. "I heard he was holed up 'round here."

"And what is his name, señor?"

"Jamison. Meriwether Jamison." Might as well tell this ape. Maybe he hated Jamison. Jamison seemed to have been pissing off lots of people lately.

But his hopes were dashed. "Ah, Don Meriwether," Navares said, smiling, showing more bad teeth. Then he stopped grinning. "He is my good friend, señor. I am sure he will be happy to meet you. I will arrange it; he is only a little farther up this canyon. But first, we will have a little ceremony. You see, señor, I am a collector."

Navares was fingering something that hung around his neck. At first Raider had taken it for some kind of grubby necklace. He looked more closely. Small shriveled objects were strung on a piece of string. Navares saw where he was looking. "My pearls," he said, holding the necklace away from his body so that Raider could see it more clearly. "Every gringo that I meet is kind enough to donate two more for me."

And then Raider realized what Navares's pearls were: severed human ears. And from the way Navares was fingering the handle of a knife he wore at his belt, Raider's ears were about to join the collection.

He thought about making a run for it, but now men were crowding closely around him, jabbing rifle barrels into his sides. To move would be to die. "Get him down from his horse," Navares snarled.

Rough hands pulled Raider's revolver from its holster, then toppled him from the saddle. He kept his balance well enough to keep from falling on his face, but it was not a particularly graceful dismount. Raider staggered for a moment, then he was seized from either side and held in place.

Navares walked toward him slowly, grinning again. He had pulled out the knife; it had a long, thin, evil blade. Navares was slowly stropping the blade against the palm of his left hand. "You have fine ears, señor," he said, his voice slightly hoarse. "They are almost as pretty as the ears of that little blonde girl. How she howled when I cut them off. Will you howl as loudly, señor?"

Navares was only a yard away now. Looking into the man's eyes, Raider realized that he was as crazy as a loon. Mean crazy. Damned if he'd let this nut cut off his ears. He braced himself, ready to tear free of the men on either side of him. The other five men were grinning just as much as Navares; clearly, they liked this ear-cutting ceremony. Looking forward to the blood, they had relaxed their guard. Raider was no longer directly covered by gun muzzles, and one of the men had a big Colt revolver stuffed into his waistband, within easy reach. Of course, they'd kill him, but maybe he'd get a couple of them first. Particularly Navares. All he needed was a slight diversion. Maybe he'd let Navares get real close with the knife, maybe he'd even let him start cutting a little—

The diversion, when it came, was decidedly less painful— for Raider. A rifle roared, and the head of the man standing next to Raider suddenly exploded, sending brains and blood flying toward Navares. A moment later a blood-curdling yell sounded from about fifty yards away, followed by a second shot, which took another of the bandits in the chest.

Not being one to look a gift horse in the mouth, Raider never even bothered to glance behind him, which was the direction from which all that shooting was coming. Instead, he ripped the revolver from the waistband of the man to his right, then shot Navares in the stomach. Navares was so close that the muzzle blast singed his shirt. Eyes wide in shock and disbelief, Navares staggered backward, the knife falling to the ground as he pressed both his hands to the hole in his belly.

Raider spun to the right, shooting the man from whom he'd taken the pistol. Only then did he get a glimpse of Jeff, riding in like an attacking Comanche, standing in his stirrups as he pumped bullets into two more bandits. Damned if the kid didn't seem to have things under control.

Raider turned back to face Navares. The bandit leader was still on his feet, sagging a little, hands still pressed to his stomach. Raider remembered what Navares had said about the little blonde girl. He stepped forward, holding the pistol out at arm's length, aiming it straight at Navares's face. "No!" Navares screamed, but his shout was cut off as Raider placed a bullet right at the bridge of his nose.

Raider spun, ready to fire again, but all the bandits were down. Most looked dead. The only one still moving didn't look like he'd live long. The kid had done some damned fine shooting.

Jeff pulled his horse to a sliding stop just a few yards from Raider, then slid to the ground, his smoking rifle still in his hand. "Are you all right?" he panted.

Raider ruefully reached up and rubbed one ear. "Yeah. All in one piece."

A gurgling cry made them both turn in time to see the last of the bandits die. Jeff looked around at all the bodies. "I did it again," he said in an awed voice. "I killed somebody."

"You did the world a favor, kid. Every one of those bastards needed killin'."

"I—I guess so," Jeff said haltingly.

Raider shuffled his feet. "You're makin' a habit of savin' my bacon, kid. 'Preciate that one hell of a lot. Anytime I can do you a favor—"

Jeff tore his eyes away from the bodies, then looked straight at Raider. "You can do one thing for me," he grated, his voice much steadier now. "You can stop calling me kid."

CHAPTER TWENTY-ONE

There was an uncomfortable silence. "Sure ki—Jeff," Raider finally said. "Guess you've earned at least that much respect."

They both might have continued standing there, self-consciously shuffling their feet, if a distant cry had not sounded from farther up the canyon. "Hey! Navares! What the hell's goin' on down there?"

"Jamison," Raider said, twisting around to look up the canyon. "Navares said he was there. He musta heard the shootin'."

Already horsemen could be seen, riding toward them. "Come on, ki—Jeff," Raider shouted. "Let's get the hell outta here!"

Raider bent down and scooped up his pistol, then both Pinkertons raced for their horses and leaped into their saddles. Jeff had just pulled his horse's head around preparatory to galloping back down the canyon, when a rifle roared from behind him. Both he and Raider could hear the meaty smack of the bullet hitting his horse. The animal screamed in agony, reared high, then fell dead. Jeff managed to kick loose from the stirrups, but nevertheless, he fell hard. Winded, half-unconscious, he tried to rise, but fell back again.

Raider guided his horse next to where Jeff was lying. "Come on!" he shouted. Jeff sat up. Raider reached down, took hold of Jeff's right hand, heaved him up onto his horse behind him, then raced for the cover of the thick brush behind the adobe.

But they had lost valuable time. The adobe was off to one side of the main trail. The delay had allowed several riders to sweep around them, making it impossible to ride back down the canyon and out into the flats. Besides, mounted double they would never have been able to outrun pursuers. "Guess we stay and fight," Raider said to Jeff. He dismounted, then helped Jeff down.

Jeff had by now regained his senses. "My rifle," he said. "Back with my horse."

"Never mind. I got two. Here. You take the Sharps."

Raider handed Jeff the big single-shot, plus a handful of its enormous cartridges, then he pulled his Winchester from its saddle scabbard. Meanwhile, they could hear men riding closer. Raider quickly scanned the terrain. The canyon wall loomed right behind them. "If we can get up into those rocks," he said, pointing to some huge boulders about a hundred feet above them, "we can hold 'em off."

Leading his horse, Raider made his way up a steep trail, Jeff following a few yards behind, facing backward. As they gained height, Jeff was able to see several horsemen milling around in front of the adobe, looking at the bodies of the dead bandits. One of the horsemen, glancing up, spotted Raider and Jeff working their way up the trail. "There they are!" the man shouted.

There were half a dozen horsemen in front of the adobe. Jeff could see others farther away. Two of the men below raised their Winchesters and opened fire. Bullets whined by, one of them hitting the saddle of Raider's horse. The horse shied in alarm, nearly tearing the reins from Raider's hands.

Jeff raised the Sharps. The range was only about a hundred and fifty yards, an easy shot for the big rifle. Kablam! One of the horsemen flew from his saddle, arms and legs windmilling. He hit the ground hard, twitched a couple of times, then lay still. Jeff flipped open the Sharps's action. The empty shell ejected, accompanied by a swirl of acrid white smoke. Jeff slid another cartridge into the chamber, then closed the action. Raising the rifle, he fired again, paying no attention to the bullets whizzing around him.

Another man was blasted from the saddle. The men below, finally realizing that Jeff's rifle easily outranged theirs, scrambled for cover. Jeff fired once more, but the big slow bullet passed behind one of the fleeing horsemen.

"Come on. Git your ass up here," Raider shouted from behind Jeff. "Or you'll git it shot off."

Jeff became aware of how much in the open he was. More shots were coming his way, better aimed shots; the men below had dismounted, and were taking more time, sighting carefully. Jeff turned and ran up the trail, ducking into the shelter of the boulders with bullets whizzing all around him.

He found Raider kneeling on the ground, peering between two of the boulders. "Seems t' be anywhere from eight to a dozen of 'em, minus the ones you plugged. They really got us bottled up."

Jeff took a look. The adobe lay below them, about a hundred yards away. The boulders they were hiding behind were situated in a little side canyon, about a hundred feet above the floor of the main canyon. They had a good vantage point for covering the adobe below, and the yard on its other side. "Trouble is," Raider muttered, "they can get 'round us over on that side."

To their left, their little canyon opened out. It would be possible for at least some of the men to work their way up the far side, outflanking them. There was heavy cover all the way. Even now Raider was pretty sure he could see movement in the brush leading to that approach. "We're gonna have to split up," he told Jeff. "One of us over there, the other here. It'll be a standoff. Maybe later, when it's dark, we can sneak on outta here."

Jeff studied the terrain on the far side of the little side canyon. There were a few boulders there, much like the ones they were hiding behind. "I'll go on over," he told Raider.

"I've got the Sharps, and the ground's a little higher. Maybe I can pick off a few more."

Raider looked over at the other boulders. "There's an open stretch the last fifty yards. I'll cover you with the Winchester. When you hear me open up, run like hell for the rocks."

Jeff nodded, then slipped away into the brush. Raider watched him go, saw how little movement there was to betray his passing. It was amazing how fast the kid—whoops—Jeff had learned. There had been nothing of the kid about him when he'd volunteered to go.

Raider surveyed the area below him. There were small movements in the brush near the adobe. He fired three carefully spaced shots with his Winchester. An answering yelp floated back up at him. He doubted he'd hurt anyone badly; the yelp had sounded too healthy, the cry of a man who'd just had the bejeezus scared out of him.

Looking toward his left, Raider caught a fleeting glimpse of Jeff, wriggling through the brush. He was about two hundred yards away; the open stretch he would have to cross lay just a few yards ahead of him.

Then Raider caught sight of other motion, in the brush just below that clear area. At least one of their besiegers had managed to slip into their little canyon!

"Jeff! Stay where you are!" Raider shouted. He raised his rifle and began to fire into the brush, where he'd seen movement. Jeff appeared to take this heavy firing for the agreed upon sign. Raider saw him break cover and race across the open ground toward the boulders above.

Cursing, Raider continued firing, but there was one place his bullets could not reach—behind a large boulder situated just below the open ground. He saw a man step out into the open, not forty yards from Jeff. The man was carrying a rifle. He raised it to his shoulder, began to aim.

Raider was aware of two things at once: not only how close the man was to Jeff, who had appaently not yet seen him, and who the man was. Jamison. It was Jamison himself.

Raider swung his rifle to the left, but he was too late.

Jamison had already fired. Raider saw smoke blossom from Jamison's rifle barrel, saw Jeff fall, one leg apparently knocked out from beneath him. Then Raider opened fire. He saw dust kick up around Jamison, but the range was too great for pinpoint shooting. Jamison scooted back behind the boulder, apparently unhurt.

Which left Jeff lying on the ground out in the open. One of his legs was bent at an unnatural angle; apparently Jamison's shot had broken the bone. Raider could see Jeff shaking his head. Then he took hold of the Sharps, and began to drag himself uphill, toward the cover of the boulders.

He had a long way to go. At his present speed, it would take him a long time. Way too long. All the way, he would be under Jamison's gunsights. Jamison called out, his voice floating up toward Raider. "You, up there. Hey you!"

"Yeah?" Raider shouted back. Anything to keep Jamison occupied. Jeff was crawling a little faster now.

"Are you the Pinkertons who were looking for me in Los Angeles?" Jamison asked.

"Yeah," Raider replied. "We're after you all right, Jamison. The entire agency. There's no way you can avoid it. We'll git you sooner or later. Why not give up, let us take you in?"

Jamison's laughter floated out from behind the rock. "And hang?"

His rifle roared. Raider could see the smoke of it coming from behind the boulder. He could also see Jeff's body convulse, could hear him cry out—and there was nothing he could do. The boulder effectively screened Jamison from his rifle.

Jamison had shot Jeff in the other leg. Jeff lay still for a moment, arms stretched in front of him, clawing at the dirt. Then he started crawling uphill again, but much more slowly.

"I recognized the kid," Jamison called out. "He put a bullet in me up north, when we hit those Basques. Now I'm putting a few in him."

"Jamison!" Raider shouted. "If you kill him, I'll kill you—real slow."

Jamison's mocking laugh came back at him. "You got it wrong, Pinkerton. You're the one who's gonna get killed. After I finish off the kid."

By now Jeff had almost made it to the cover of the boulders, leaving a trail of blood behind him. Raider saw the barrel of Jamison's rifle protrude from behind his own boulder. "So long, kid," he heard Jamison shout.

Raider fired madly, trying to hit the tiny dark line of that rifle barrel. He watched helplessly as smoke blossomed from it again, saw Jeff's body jerk, stiffen, go limp, then roll loosely down the slope, finally coming to a stop against a small rock. Then Jeff lay still.

A moment's silence followed. Finally Raider spoke, almost in a conversational tone, but in the dry mountain air his voice carried clearly. "Jamison, you're a dead man," he said clamly.

Jamison's laugh floated back up to him, but less convincingly this time. There was a note of worry in it, as if the very calmness of Raider's statement, the certainty of it, had rattled him.

Raider reloaded his Winchester, then stuffed his pockets full of extra shells. He looked out between the boulders again. Nothing seemed to have changed; Jamison was probably still behind the boulder that sheltered him, while his men had remained below, hidden in the brush on the other side of the adobe. From time to time they'd fired up at him, but for the most part they had been caught up in the drama of watching Jamison kill Jeff.

Raider slipped away into the brush, to his right. When he had to, he could move like an Indian, and he did so now, crawling for a while, then, at another point, where there was better cover, running bent over. Within ten minutes he had worked his way around to the right side of the adobe. Lying on his stomach behind some brush, he stopped to reconnoiter.

Jamison gave him some unintended help. "Hey, Jesse," Jamison called out. "Have you seen anything move up there lately?"

"Naw," a voice replied from quite close to Raider. Great. Jesse, whoever he was, had pinpointed his location.

Raider slipped through the brush for another twenty yards. Finally he stopped; he could hear the mutter of voices a little way ahead. Several men. Then he saw them, vague forms visible through the brush, some sitting, others kneeling as they looked upward, one man actually standing, probably Jesse, shading his eyes as he studied the boulders where Raider was supposedly hiding.

Raider stood up and walked forward, Winchester ready. Since none of the beseigers suspected he might have gotten around behind them, nobody reacted—until Raider's bullet blew apart Jesse's head.

Firing, moving, always firing, Raider tore the men to pieces with his Winchester. There were five of them, but only two managed to fire in return, shots that missed badly, because they were already reeling under the impact of Raider's bullets. Raider levered his rifle dry, over twenty shots. Most of them found flesh. Within seconds of his appearance all five men were dead, expressions of horror and surprise frozen forever onto their faces.

Raider quickly began to reload. He was shoving in the last cartridge when a man came bursting out of the brush, firing a pistol at Raider. Raider, who'd had the foresight to lever a cartridge into the chamber as soon as he'd begun reloading, shot the man down with two well-aimed shots.

Raider quickly began adding in his head. Six. He'd killed six. Jeff had killed two with the Sharps. That meant eight. Adding Jamison, nine men were accounted for. But he'd been sure there were at least ten. Were there more men hiding in the brush?

He got his answer when he heard a horse grunt under sudden weight, followed by muffled cursing, then the pounding of hooves. Someone was running a horse hard. Raider took a chance on standing up. Sure enough, a mounted man was racing away from the adobe at high speed, headed down-canyon, obviously riding for his life. Probably the last of them, except for Jamison.

Raider heard Jamison then, calling from his vantage point above. "Hey! Hey, down there. Jesse. Hank. What was all that shooting? Did you get him?"

Raider crawled into the cover of the adobe. "Jesse's not gonna answer, Jamison," he called out. "Hank neither. They're dead, Jamison, all of 'em are dead, 'cept for the one who had the brains to hightail it outta here."

"Son of a bitch!"

Raider could hear Jamison's involuntary exclamation quite clearly. There was just the slightest touch of panic in Jamison's voice.

"Now I'm comin' for you, Jamison," Raider shouted. "Comin' t' kill you, just like I promised. Because of what you did t' the kid."

"Now, wait a minute," Jamison called out.

"Too late for waitin', Jamison. Too late for surrender. You're a dead man. I already told you that."

He heard sulfurous cursing coming from Jamison's position, but by then Raider was already in motion, crawling at first, then leaping erect to race across a small patch of open ground, heading toward Jamison's nest of boulders. Jamison fired, but wildly, his bullets missing Raider by a wide margin.

Raider did not care about bullets; he was in the grip of an unthinking madness, his mind was full of ugly images of the way Jeff had crawled for his life, and of the mockery Jamison had made of the kid's effort, killing him just a few feet from safety.

The boulders were just ahead now. Raider raced for them. Just as he was about to gain their cover, Jamison appeared, rifle ready. He fired first. The bullet hit the stock of Raider's rifle, tearing it from his grip. "Now!" Jamison shouted triumphantly, raising his own rifle, aiming straight at Raider's chest.

There was no way he could miss; the range was only about twenty yards. Raider's hands were still tingling from the impact of Jamison's bullet against his rifle. For just one moment, he was helpless, and Jamison was about to take advantage of that helplessness. With mounting fury, Raider stared into Jamison's gloating face.

Click. The hammer of Jamison's rifle came down on an empty chamber. Cursing, Jamison threw the rifle away, then reached for his pistol.

Raider was also reaching for his pistol, but his numbed hand was a trifle slow. Jamison was able to fire first, but Jamison was rattled, and his bullet went too far to the side, hitting Raider's upper left arm. It was just a flesh wound, but the impact of the big bullet was enough to spin Raider around. He spun all the way, his gun hand held high as he fought to regain his balance. As he finished the spin he saw that Jamison was about to fire again. There would be no time to bring his hand down, cock the pistol, and fire, so he simply threw it, threw his pistol straight at Jamison, who instinctively raised his arms to ward it off. The pistol hit Jamison in the face, sending him staggering backward. Raider launched himself forward, following his pistol. He kicked high, the toe of his boot knocking the pistol from Jamison's hand.

The two men, both winded, stood facing one another for a moment, each of them unarmed, except for their knives. "Time to die, Jamison," Raider said coldly. Drawing his bowie, he started forward. Jamison fumbled for his own knife; it was the kind called by some an Arkansas toothpick, with a narrow but heavy blade that tapered to a needle-sharp point. More of a dagger than a knife. An excellent killing machine.

Blood ran down Jamison's face from where Raider's pistol had hit him. He backed away; Raider's steady advance had filled him with fear. Raider flexed his left arm. It hurt, and would hurt one hell of a lot more later—if he lived. But he could still use it for balance.

He moved another step forward, with the heavy, foot-long blade held out in front of him. Jamison took another step backward; Raider could see that he was trying to get to the pistol that had been kicked out of his hand, but Raider crowded in close, forcing Jamison to defend himself.

Changing direction, Jamison launched himself forward, thrusting at Raider's stomach. The sudden change of tactics almost succeeded, but at the last moment Raider's bowie beat the lighter blade aside, then Raider cut, slashing a shallow wound in Jamison's right forearm.

Jamison fell back, clasping his left hand over the wound. He doesn't like being cut, Raider thought, so he leaped forward, slashing his bowie in big arcs. Caught by surprise, Jamison staggered backward, holding up his left arm for defense. Raider cut a slash nearly the length of the arm, then, as Jamison screamed in pain, struck hard with his knife, severing Jamison's left hand.

Jamison stood for a moment, staring dumbly at the stump, which was spouting blood. Finally, screaming an unintelligible curse, he launched himself at Raider in one final wild attack.

Raider, having anticipated the timing, simply took hold of Jamison's right wrist, then stepped in close and drove his knife hard into Jamison's belly, low down, near the pelvis. Jamison grunted, his eyes bulging, more in shock than in pain.

The faces of both men were only inches apart. Raider looked straight into Jamison's panicked eyes. "That was for all the people you robbed an' killed," he said. "An' this is for what you did t' Jeff, for the way you killed him."

He turned the blade, then ripped it upward, hard. The pain came, overwhelming pain, and Jamison screamed, a high, keening scream that echoed and reechoed among the rocks. He dropped his knife and began to slowly double up. Raider stepped backward, withdrawing his blade. A gout of blood washed over his hand, hot and sticky.

Raider walked over to a patch of grass, where he cleaned his hands and knife blade. Then he sat down on a rock to watch Jamison die. It did not take long; by now Jamison had lost so much blood that he was weakening fast. His eyes full of fear, he sat, panting, trying to hold in his guts. A spasm wracked his body, and he screamed. The scream used up the last of his strength. Grunting, he fell forward onto his face. Gradually, his limbs relaxed. When his panting stopped with a rattling gasp, Raider knew that he was dead.

Raider felt very tired. As he'd sat and watched, the reality of Jamison's death had brought him no real satisfaction. Nothing had happened that would bring Jeff back. Images of that open, boyish, trusting face kept intruding. A face that would smile no more. He looked upslope, where the bundle of rags that used to be Jeff was lying. Slowly, Raider got to his feet, trying to make up his mind whether he should bury Jeff here, where he fell, or take his body back to Los Angeles.

A hell of a way to make a living. But the only way he knew.

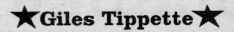